D0016172

Presented to:
FROM
OCCASION
DATE

Dec. 8, 20

With love to

Mom & Dad

Gompa & Grammy

Our parents give us wings —
but our grandparents
give us roots

Conifer, Colorado

FOCUS ON THE FAMILY®
presents

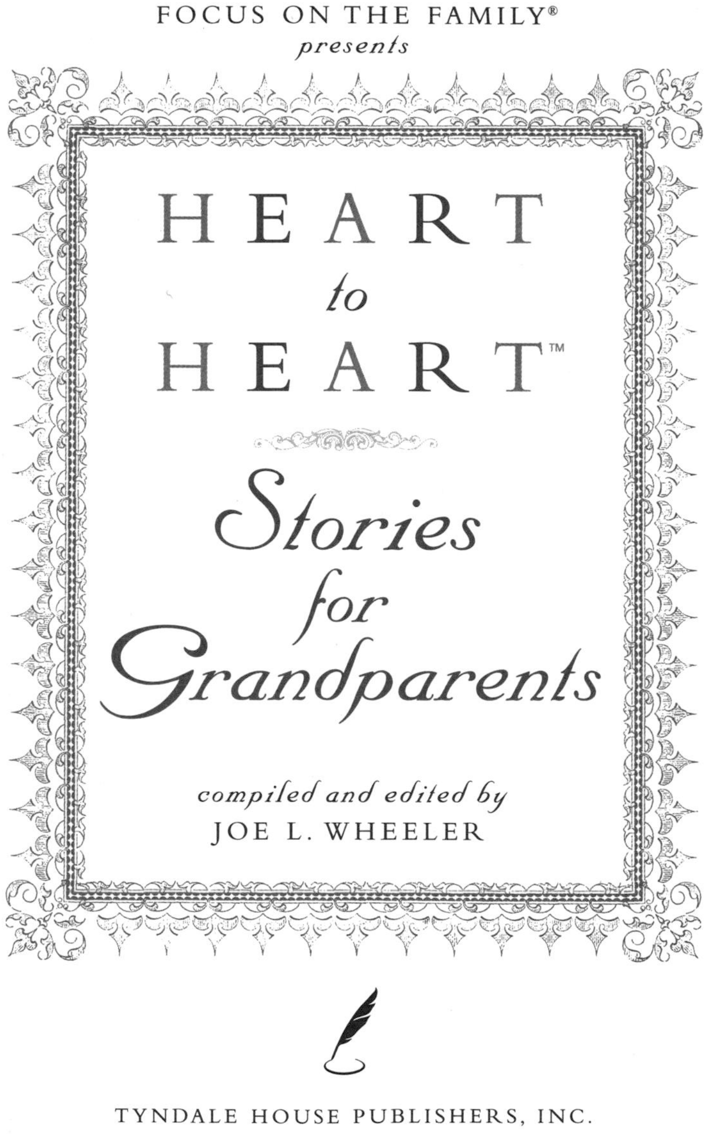

HEART *to* HEART™

Stories for Grandparents

compiled and edited by
JOE L. WHEELER

TYNDALE HOUSE PUBLISHERS, INC.
WHEATON, ILLINOIS

Visit Tyndale's exciting Web site at www.tyndale.com

A Focus on the Family book published by Tyndale House Publishers, Inc.

Designed by Jenny Swanson

Woodcut illustrations are from the library of Joe L. Wheeler.

Illustration on page 174 by Gale Keith. Used by permission of Scholastic Press.

Published in association with the literary agency of Alive Communications, 7680 Goddard Street, Suite 200, Colorado Springs, CO 80920.

Scripture quotations are taken from the *Holy Bible,* King James Version.

Library of Congress Cataloging-in-Publication Data

Heart to heart : stories for grandparents / compiled and edited by Joe L. Wheeler.
p. cm. — (Heart to heart series)
ISBN 0-8423-5379-8
1. Grandparents—Fiction. 2. Grandparent and child—Fiction. 3. Domestic fiction, American.
I. Wheeler, Joe L. II. Series.
PS648.G73 S76 2002
813′.01083520432—dc21 2002001245

Printed in Italy

08 07 06 05 04 03 02
7 6 5 4 3 2 1

Once upon a time almost every child in America was blessed—
as I was—with three great gifts, three sanctuaries to retreat to:
the home of one's parents, the home of one's paternal grandparents,
and the home of one's maternal grandparents. Now,
no small thanks to the ravages of divorce,
those three sanctuaries are no longer a given.

But I had them. My father's parents, in their Howell Mountain
Shangri-la high above the Napa Valley, complete with roses and
ferns in Grandma's rock garden, and thousands of apple trees in
Grandpa's far-flung orchards. My mother's parents, in their Humboldt
County three-story home, complete with acres of fuchsias and
asters in the nursery gardens below the house, and towering
redwoods fading into the mists in the hills behind.

I am very much a part of those two beloved couples who transmitted
their family history and values to me. Thus it gives me great pleasure to
dedicate this book to the late

ROLLO AND RUBY WHEELER
of
ANGWIN, CALIFORNIA

and

HERBERT AND JOSEPHINE LEININGER
of
ARCATA, CALIFORNIA

CONTENTS

ACKNOWLEDGMENTS

Introduction: "Roots to Our Wings," by Joseph Leininger Wheeler. Copyright © 2002. Printed by permission of the author.

"When Tulips Die in the Spring," by Ruth Garren. Published in *Insight's Most Unforgettable Stories* (Hagerstown, Md.: Review and Herald Publishing Association, 1990). Reprinted by permission of the publisher and the author.

"You Can't Do It, Grandma!" by Frank L. Hicks, Jr. Published in *Sunshine Magazine,* July 1977. Reprinted by permission of Garth Henrichs, publisher of Sunshine Publications. If anyone can provide knowledge of where the author (or author's next-of-kin) can be found, please send to Joe L. Wheeler (P.O. Box 1246, Conifer, CO, 80433).

"The Heart's Beginning," by Pearl S. Buck. Published in *Woman's Home Companion,* December 1954. Copyright © 1954 by Pearl S. Buck. Copyright renewed 1982. Reprinted by permission of Harold Ober Associates, Inc.

"Bread Crusts," by Louise Seymour Hasbrouck. Published in *The Youth's Instructor,* July 6, 1926. Reprinted by permission of Joe Wheeler (P.O. Box 1246, Conifer, CO 80433) and Review and Herald Publishing Association, Hagerstown, MD.

"His First Dress Suit," by Felicia Buttz Clark. Published in *The Youth's Instructor,* December 1918. Text reprinted by permission of Joe Wheeler (P.O. Box 1246, Conifer, CO 80433) and Review and Herald Publishing Association, Hagerstown, MD.

"Amy's Butterfly," by Kathryn Smith Boyette. Published in *Sunshine Magazine,* August 1982. Reprinted by permission of Garth Henrichs, publisher of Sunshine Publications. If anyone can provide knowledge of where the author (or author's next-of-kin) can be found, please send to Joe L. Wheeler (P.O. Box 1246, Conifer, CO, 80433).

"Practice Hours," by Agnes Barden Dustin. If anyone can provide knowledge of earliest publication of this old story, please send that information to Joe Wheeler (P.O. Box 1246, Conifer, CO 80433).

"His Legacy," by Bill Gaither. Published in *I Almost Missed the Sunset* by William Gaither with Jerry B. Jenkins. Copyright © 1992 by William J. Gaither. All rights controlled by Gaither Copyright Management. This text reprinted with permission from *The Reader's Digest*, May 1992. Copyright © 1992 by *The Reader's Digest Association, Inc.*

"The Cousins' Conspiracy," by Helen Ward Banks. Published in *St. Nicholas Magazine,* February 1925.

"The Delayed Letter," by Elizabeth Ann Tollmann. Published in *The Youth's Instructor,* August 24, 1920. Text reprinted by permission of Joe L. Wheeler (P.O. Box 1246, Conifer, CO 80433) and Review and Herald Publishing Association, Hagerstown, MD.

"Ready for Heaven," by Ewart A. Autry. Reprinted by permission of Lola M. Autry.

"An Old-Fashioned Love Story," by Betty Steele Everett. Published in *Sunshine Magazine,* May 1981. Reprinted by permission of Garth Henrichs, publisher of Sunshine Publications. If anyone can provide knowledge of where the author (or author's next-of-kin) can be found, please send to Joe L. Wheeler (P.O. Box 1246, Conifer, CO, 80433).

"A Gift for Lauren," by Denise Anderson Boiko. Published by permission of the author.

"The Mason Family on Exhibition," author unknown. If anyone can provide knowledge of authorship and earliest publication of this old story, please send that information to Joe L. Wheeler (P.O. Box 1246, Conifer, CO 80433).

"One Breath Away," by Alfred F. Eckhardt. Published by permission of the author.

"The Guest of Honor," by Mabel McKee. Published in *Young People's Weekly,* February 13, 1932. Reprinted by permission of Joe L. Wheeler (P.O. Box 1246, Conifer, CO 80433); David C. Cook Ministries, Colorado Springs, CO; and Fleming H. Revell, a division of Baker Book House, Grand Rapids, MI.

"The Elk Tooth Dress," by Dorothy Johnson. Copyright © 1957 by Dorothy Johnson. Reprinted by permission of McIntosh and Otis, Inc.

"The Magician," by John M. Hebert. Published in *Sunshine Magazine,* November 1983. Reprinted by permission of Garth Henrichs, publisher of Sunshine Publications. If anyone can provide knowledge of where the author (or author's next-of-kin) can be found, please send to Joe L. Wheeler (P.O. Box 1246, Conifer, CO, 80433).

"Grandmother's End of the Ice Cream," by Annie Hamilton Donnell. Published in *The Youth's Instructor,* June 12, 1923. Reprinted by permission of Joe Wheeler (P.O. Box 1246, Conifer, CO 80433) and Review and Herald Publishing Association, Hagerstown, MD.

"The Shabby Little House," by Irene S. Woodcock. Published in *The Youth's Instructor,* April 15, 1924. Reprinted by permission of Joe L. Wheeler (P.O. Box 1246, Conifer, CO 80433) and Review and Herald Publishing Association, Hagerstown, MD.

"The Super-Duper," by Mary Kay Thompson. Published in *Sunshine Magazine,* September 1980. Reprinted by permission of Garth Henrichs, publisher of Sunshine

ALMANAC

Introduction

ROOTS TO OUR WINGS: GRANDPARENTING

Joseph Leininger Wheeler

THE BOND BETWEEN US

Reflection comes with age. Children, living as they do only in God's time—the eternal present—consider the past irrelevant. As for the future, children consider tomorrow to be a forever away from today. Young people all too often forsake the present for the past or the future. But their lexicon holds far more regret than reflection. In fact, so rare is silence in their lives that reflection rarely occurs at all. Young adults, especially those who are married and have children and careers, are akin to eternal-motion machines, and mistakenly assume that mere motion is synonymous with progress or growth. Rarely do they find even a few moments in which to reflect.

But eventually there comes a time when the sand in one's hourglass is disproportionately below the funnel rather than above. A time when careers lose their earlier power over us and become "thou mays" instead of "thou shalts." Serendipitously, it is also at this wondrous time that many of us become this unanticipated and unplanned thing lexicographers label "grandparents."

God planned it this way—planned the age of reflection to synchronize with the age of grandparenting. For good measure, God also chose this period of our lives to release us from bondage to those erstwhile tormentors, hormones (whose very nature precludes coexistence with either reason or reflection).

Right at this time, something happens: the telephone rings.

"Mom, I've got a question for you."

"Y-e-s?"

"Do you have any firm plans for the second week in February?"

"N-o. Why?"

"Well, uh . . . I . . . uh . . . might need you then."

And so we learn that the God of miracles has one in store just for us—a miracle quite different from that of our own children and, in some ways, more uniquely ours.

"Come now!" I can hear you retort. "How can anything be more ours than our own children?"

There is a unique emotional connection between grandparent and grandchild that no one can truly explain. However, a scientific perspective on that question is found in a book two-thirds of a century old: famed gynecologist Dr. Frederic Loomis's insightful *The Bond between Us*. It's too bad the nine justices of the U.S. Supreme Court didn't weigh in this book as evidence in their recent ruling on the rights of grandparents. Had they done so, their ruling might well have been different.

Here are perhaps the most revolutionary and staggering words ever written on the subject of grandparenting:

> Tucked away in a special place for safe-keeping, as in a safety deposit box in a bank, is a special kind of cell which behaves in a very different way. These cells are not, in a large sense, parts of our own bodies at all—just something handed to us by our parents to keep in trust. When a baby girl is born, in fact long before she is born, all the characteristics for better or worse which she can pass on to her babies are already hidden away within her in a highly specialized area, the ovary; and in a somewhat different way, a father can pass on only those possibilities he had when he was born, a mixture of all he had received from his father and mother. So in a sense we are really the children of our grandparents, since a man cannot produce a new variety of sperm and a woman can never change the little basket of eggs which came into the world at the same time she did.[1]

In truth, then, as Dr. Loomis tells us, we are not only the children of our parents but we are also in some sense the children of our *grandparents,* both being responsible for our characteristics, psyche, and DNA. This sheds light on that mystic bonding between grandparent and grandchild, the ultimate soulmates. It

[1] *Frederic Loomis,* The Bond between Us *(New York: Alfred A. Knopf, 1942), 133–134. In December 2001 I shared this quotation with Ellen Mulhern, M.D., OB-GYN, and she confirmed that Dr. Loomis's words are just as true today as when they were first written.*

may even explain why grandparents tend to accept their grandchildren just as they are even if they failed to do that with their own children.

WHAT A PARADOX!

One of the very strangest ironies, without question: At the very time of life when cataracts are likely to cloud one's external vision, the cataracts are removed from one's inner vision. Long ago the poet Wordsworth reminded us that we generally fail to see clearly that which is too close to us.

> The world is too much with us; late and soon,
> Getting and spending, we lay waste our powers. . . .[2]

When a 737 leaves the runway, the passengers gain a perspective of the world denied those who observe it only from ground level. So it is with children. Observed too close, we see them only as separate cels—like those single frames of celluloid used in animation. Only at a distance may the cels be connected and animation take place. Thus a child may be changing every day into something better or something worse, and the parent fails to perceive it. But a grandparent, blessed by two levels of perspective (the external—gained by seeing the children less frequently—and the kind gained only by looking backward through the prism of time), is likely to see such changes almost instantly.

But there is another, even more significant reason, for grandparents' greater clarity of vision. Whereas the parents can see only the early frames of the movie of their lives flashed on a screen for contemplation, the grandparents are almost to the end of the

[2] *William Wordsworth, "The World Is Too Much with Us; Late and Soon"*

movie of *their* lives. They know how the show is going to play out, and more significantly, they know *why*. Such knowledge and awareness come too late in life for grandparents to avert the consequences of their own acts (both of commission and omission), but not too late to try to avert the repetition of such consequences in the lives of their grandchildren.

In this respect, saddest of all may be the "Cassandra" grandparent, so called for the Cassandra of Greek mythology who was given the gift of prophecy but then cursed so that no one would believe the true words she spoke. The "Cassandra" grandparent is doomed to see wise counsel rejected, but for a different reason from the original Cassandra: because the counsel is so contrary to the life already lived that the recipient considers it to be merely sour grapes or an attempt to deprive a descendant of the chance to make such mistakes on his or her own.

Even so, wise is the grandchild who accepts such hard-earned counsel, knowing how high a price was paid for it.

LIBRARIES BURNING DOWN

Sadly, America is somewhat unique among the world's nations in its obsession with the cult of youth. Age is something we fear with every atom of our being. Like Oscar Wilde's Dorian Gray, we will resort to almost anything rather than reveal the ravages of our acts and years for the world to see. In much of the rest of the world, society values and reveres those who have achieved the wisdom that comes only with years. Blessed beyond measure are those who live in such societies.

One might hope that the turn of the millennium will bring about change in this respect. Perhaps George W. Bush's choosing cabinet members for their experience and wisdom rather than their youth is a precursor of societal change. (The significance of this act has come home to us all in the wake of the tragic World Trade Center conflagration on September 11, 2001.) We as a society have paid a terrible price for our rejection of those who have gained wisdom with the passing of years. We have taken one of God's greatest gifts—the interrelationship of generations that once made America so strong—and replaced it with gated communities that wall out intergenerational communication. Where once three generations lived in the same vicinity and interacted from day to day so that each age level was influenced by the others, today we interact very little.

What we fail to take into consideration is the inexorable continuity of life, life's remorseless insistence on coming full circle. Perhaps the most apt expression of this principle of human behavior is found in an oft-repeated story: A father is forced by circumstances to live with his son's family. Because the father no longer has an income of his own, he is treated more as an unwelcome beggar than an honored and beloved father. Eventually the father reaches the point where he loses some of his social graces, and he spills food on himself because of unsteady hands. Disgusted, his son exiles his father to a back room and dumps his food into a trough rather than a dish since "he'll only spill it anyhow"—and this way no one else will be forced to watch him do it. The rest of the story most of us have already heard: One day the son hears some hammering and decides to find out where it's coming from. He discovers his own little son hammering some small boards together. When asked what he's making, the boy innocently explains, "I'm making a trough for you so it'll be ready when you get old like Grandpa."

There is virtual certainty that life will repeat itself. As we treat an aged parent, so our children will later treat us. There are almost no exceptions to this rule.

They say that when an elderly person dies, it's like a library burning down. All that lifetime's accumulation of wisdom and memories dies also with that last breath. And nowhere is such a loss felt more keenly than among family. Who among us has not regretted waiting too long to get Mother to identify the faces in those old photographs? Now no one will ever know!

Today we face even crueler enemies than death: Alzheimer's disease and dementia. It is said that those of us who reach age sixty-five will run a high risk of eventually succumbing to either Alzheimer's or some form of dementia ourselves, or having it manifested in the life of one very close and very dear to us. One of my cherished friends, Nancy Rue, has just written a book titled *Pascal's Wager* that deals with such a case. What do we do when the mind of a dear one clouds over? How do we treat such a person? Nancy takes us to her implied conclusion: In such cases, we must recognize that, hidden in the fog and vacuity, is still that person's soul, tenderly cared for by its Maker and eventual Receiver, God.

But every day we can avail ourselves of the opportunity to connect with our families while there is yet time, to chronicle those memories, to tell those stories while they are still remembered, to identify those old photos. Most of all, to treasure each day we have together and take every opportunity to sit at each other's feet and learn, grow, and become. To take full advantage—either on the delivering or receiving end—of God's great gift of grandparenting. To recognize that while our parents may give us wings, it is our grandparents who give us roots. Our grandparents, who alone can show us where home is.

THIS COLLECTION

Into this book I have poured the greatest grandparenting stories I have ever come across. Not surprisingly, not as many such stories are being written today as was true during the golden age of Judeo-Christian stories (1880s–1950s).

Featured in this collection are such well-known names as Annie Hamilton Donnell, Mabel McKee, Helen Ward Banks, Felicia Buttz Clark, Bill Gaither, Dorothy Johnson, and Pearl S. Buck.

CODA

I invite you to search out other stories of equal power, stories that move you deeply and that illustrate the values upon which this nation was founded. Many of these stories will be old, but others may be new. If you send me copies of the ones that have meant the most to you and your family, please include the author, publisher, and date of first publication if at all possible. With your help we will be able to put together additional collections (centered on other topics) for home, church, and school. You may reach me by writing to:

Joe L. Wheeler, Ph.D.
Tyndale House Publishers
c/o Editorial Department
P.O. Box 80
Wheaton, Illinois 60189-0080

May the Lord bless and guide the ministry of these stories in your home.

WHEN TULIPS DIE IN THE SPRING

Ruth Garren

When Jenny asked her mother why she didn't just tear out the dead, ugly tulips in the garden, Mom answered, "Because it's not time yet. They have to die down completely; then you can just pull the stems out of the ground." But Jenny was to discover that there was another application for that statement—strangely enough, one that had to do with fiddling on Old Timers' Day.

Only nine o'clock in the morning, and already it was hot. Jenny looked out of her bedroom window. The fields and trees around the house had gone from spring green to the deeper green of summer in one rainless May week.

Her grandfather, whom everyone called Papa John, was working in the garden. She could hear the *tick tick* of his hoe against the dry earth, and a few birds chirping.

Last week Jenny had gotten out of school for the summer. Already she knew it was going to be long.

She turned from the window to her dresser, which was covered with trophies: six years of Presidential Fitness Awards; a handful of ribbons from Field Day events at school; seven firsts, three seconds, and one grand prize trophy for fiddling in Mountain Youth festivals.

She picked up the newspaper clippings from the Benton *Beacon,* sealed in plastic to keep them from yellowing. Jenny was five years old in the photograph, and her great-grandfather, whom she'd always called Grandpa, was seventy-five. The photographer had caught the two of them, dappled in sunlight through the leaves of a huge oak tree, holding their fiddles and smiling into each other's faces.

The paper read: "Five-year-old Jenny Burrows is a fifth-generation fiddler. Her great-grandfather Clive Sprague, of Benton, and his brother Gus, of Hiwassee, were taught by their father when they were about Jenny's age. Clive, in turn, taught his daughter Helen (now deceased) and his grandson Philip, Jenny's father, who died in Vietnam. 'Jenny's got real talent,' Mr. Sprague comments. 'You've either got it or you don't, and Jenny's got more of it than any young'un I've ever taught—in or out of the family.' Jenny's mother plays the mandolin. Other family members play the bass fiddle, guitar, and banjo. The family group entertains regularly in the Polk County area. Look for them on Old Timers' Day at Big Ridge Park at the same spot under the big oak where family members have gathered a crowd on Old Timers' Day for seventy years."

Jenny studied the photograph. Grandpa's face was crisscrossed with lines. Now the lines had turned to furrows, giving his face character and making him a natural subject for the photographers who showed up at every Old Timers' Day.

Jenny set the clipping back on the dresser. *Well, they're in for a surprise this year,* she thought, *because Jenny Burrows, award-winning fiddler, will not be fiddling on Old Timers' Day. She's had enough.* She tied her hair back with a ribbon to lift it from her neck.

Jenny went outside. Her mother was digging holes in the dirt and planting flowers. A drop of sweat balanced on the tip of her nose. Streaks of dirt showed where she had wiped her forehead.

"You look like you've been out here awhile," Jenny said.

"A couple of hours."

"And you're going to get one of those redneck tans again, Mom. Just like last year."

"Well, Jenny, the only way to avoid that is to work outside in my bathing suit, and I don't believe I'll be doing that."

Again this spring Mom was mixing petunias and impatiens, snapdragons and begonias, without much thought for color or design.

"Mom," Jenny asked her, not for the first time, "why don't you do all pink things, or all pink and white? This is going to look like a crazy quilt."

"Well, honey, it's the way I like it."

Jenny knew she would say that.

"Mom, I want to talk to you about something."

"Go right ahead."

"I don't want to play for Old Timers' Day Sunday."

"Why not?"

"Because I don't play the fiddle anymore."

"Since when?"

"Since now. I'm beginning to get good on the violin, and I don't want to get myself mixed up."

"What does your teacher say about that?"

"Nothing. He doesn't know I play the fiddle."

"You mean to tell me you've been taking lessons from him for two years and you didn't tell him?"

"No."

"And he's never caught on?"

"No."

"He never thought you were a bit gifted for a beginner?"

"He said I had good tone for a beginner, but I just said thank you and let him teach me technique and everything else, just like I'd never held a bow or a violin before."

"Well, Jenny Burrows—" the spade was furiously stabbing the earth—"that is deceitful. That is right next door to an outright lie. Do you think your grandmother would have done that, or your father?"

"I don't know, and I don't care. Fiddling is a hokey thing to do, anyway."

"Hokey? Where did you get that idea? You are going to break your great-grandfather's heart, young lady, and your Uncle Gus's, too."

"They'll get over it."

"They're in their eighties. They may not have another Old Timers' Day."

"You're trying to lay guilt on me, Mom. I hate it when you

do that. Grandpa and Uncle Gus might as well get used to playing without me. Besides, there's Uncle Gus's family."

"But they've never been as good as you are, and they never will be. And you know it." Mom paused a minute and stood up to confront Jenny at eye level. "You know you can't put your 'hokey' mountain traditions behind you any more than you can deny the fact that you're a fourth-generation Christian."

"Well, the jury is still out on that one."

"Jenny Burrows!" her mother said, shocked.

"What are those ugly things there?" Jenny asked, trying to change a subject she wished she'd never started.

"Those are the last of the tulips."

"Why don't you dig them out?"

"Because it's not time yet. They have to die down completely; then you can just pull the stems out of the ground. I figure I'll put these impatiens there, and pretty soon they'll be big enough so you won't even notice the tulips."

"I'd pull them out."

"I know you would."

Old Timers' Day dawned bright and clear, the kind of weather Jenny used to pray for in the old days. In the kitchen her mom was packing sandwiches and potato salad into the cooler. Mom's mandolin and Jenny's fiddle stood at the back door, ready to be carried to Papa John's van.

"My fiddle's there," Jenny pointed out. "I told you not to pack it."

"It's Papa's van, Jenny, and he'll take it if he wants to."

"Well, do what you want, but you're just taking up space for nothing."

The scene at Big Ridge Park was as noisy, colorful, and confusing as past summers. Some groups were already playing music. Others were standing around talking. People who had come to listen waited with their lawn chairs to see which groups might be worthy of their sitting-down attention.

Grandpa began tuning up. Papa John, who said he'd married his wife, Helen, to get music genes into his family, not because he had any talent to bring to hers, sat in a chair in the shade. He and Helen had had only one child, Philip. Philip and Madge had had only Jenny, and only Jenny was left.

The music began. Grandpa led with a slow, gentle ballad. Jenny noticed that his fingers were stiff and his tone no longer as warm or rich as she remembered it. Still, he was one of the best fiddlers around.

Then someone asked for "Foggy Mountain Breakdown," a fast-clogging number. Grandpa started out playing first fiddle, but his fingers faltered. He nodded toward Gus's son Axel. Axel took over, fumbling a little in the beginning, but not doing too badly. Still, Jenny could see the frustration on Grandpa's face. He was used to being the best.

Jenny remembered how in the old days, when she was just learning, Grandpa's expertise had covered for her immature playing. Could she do any less for him?

She went to the van and got her fiddle. She tuned it as she walked back, holding the instrument, made by Grandpa himself, gently under her chin. She slid in at the edge of the group and began playing second fiddle with Grandpa, her bowing sure and strong, her tone as mellow as his had been in his best years.

He nodded to her, and she took the lead. Her fingers had

become stronger and more flexible from violin lessons and typing classes. The music filtered up among the leaves of the oak tree and wafted off toward the mountains that made up Big Ridge. People set their lawn chairs down to relax and listen and watch.

Jenny was taking over for her great-grandfather, covering his weak tones with her strong ones as he had once done for her. Yes, it was right *not* to pull out the tulips—her roots. As the cameras clicked, she again smiled up into Grandpa's furrowed face.

Ruth Garren

Ruth Garren, freelance writer and publicist, today writes from eastern Tennessee.

YOU CAN'T DO IT, GRANDMA!

Frank L. Hicks, Jr.

Just because she was seventy-six and a grandmother, they said she couldn't do it. Obstinately, she determined to hike the trail by herself anyway.

Who says a seventy-six-year-old grandmother can't hike the Bright Angel Trail down to the floor of one of the natural wonders of the world, the Grand Canyon? Well, my two granddaughters, my daughter, a forest ranger, various park officials, and assorted onlookers were certainly making a very good attempt at it. As we approached the trailhead at the canyon's edge, we found a crowd of fifty or sixty spectators. I felt more awed by the attention I was receiving than by the canyon.

"Grandma, you can't, you just can't do it. Grandmothers can't do things like this, and you'll just look foolish and make us feel ridiculous." Cindy was noticeably irritated by my unorthodox behavior.

But to tell a seventy-six-year-old grandmother she can't do something because she looks foolish is to dare her to do it—at least if she's a rebellious grandmother like me. There's a mischievous pleasure in being a rebel. I think senior citizens have something in common with the younger generation in that regard.

Several young backpackers making a final check of their gear seemed to find the whole situation amusing and watched with suppressed laughter. Gail, my other granddaughter, said I looked like something out of *It's a Mad, Mad, Mad, Mad World* with my borrowed backpack of ancient vintage and assorted paraphernalia clinging precariously to strings and ropes all over it, akin to the old pots-and-pans peddlers.

All activity ceased as I reached the canyon edge. One "well-wisher" was giving 50:1 odds I'd never get a mile down the trail, and 100:1 I'd never come out alive. The disheartening fact was that he couldn't find anyone to accept his bet.

"Please, Mother, if you persist in this stupid folly, at least ride a mule down the trail. You're no kid anymore. Be sensible; this just isn't proper."

But seventy-six-year-old grandmothers are not always sensible and proper when their descendants tell them they have to be. I had to be sensible for too many years while raising a family; now it was my turn to rebel. This grandmother was going to be free even if it killed her, which seemed to be the reason for the concern.

Happiness is watching the astonished looks on people's faces when you start to do something they've just told you is impossible. I felt like Lindbergh and Columbus rolled into one.

So with childish glee and a wave I simply turned and strolled off down the trail, my gear swaying ominously from side to side. Clickety-clacks from cameras and several foreboding whispers were all that competed with the early-morning silence as I started my descent.

Canyon walls quickly swallowed up my audience and my doubts. The canyon itself revealed a personality all its own. Its beauty and immensity were truly overwhelming.

There were some moments of near disaster, and others of moving inspiration. About a mile down into the canyon the shoulder harness on the right side of my backpack suddenly broke, dumping me unceremoniously into an unfriendly cactus and scattering my equipment.

I could think only of turning back: I had failed. But several teenage girls coming up the trail soon rounded up my gear, and together we rigged a makeshift strap out of rope. Only their cheerful optimism kept me going. Within an hour I was again bobbing along the trail, still heading down.

One of the most inspiring moments of the trip occurred when I reached the roaring Colorado River at the very bottom of the canyon and crossed the little bridge. I nicknamed it the Jordan and truly felt that I had been reborn in a new and promised land.

Camping on the bottom among the young people was another thrill. I was accepted as one of the group. The years melted away, although my old bones did protest against sleeping on hard ground.

But, with apologies to Newton, all that goes down must come back up, and going down was nothing compared to climbing back. Now muscles I had lost track of sixty years ago threatened to go on strike, while my legs were on the verge of a sit-down demonstration. The medieval rack would have felt like a lounge chair in comparison.

As the day wore on, I wore out. Blisters I got going down were raising their own crop on the way up. To say I was exhausted would be the century's greatest understatement. Still, my adventure had to continue. Every once in a while a very tired inner voice would plead, *What's a nice old gal like you doing in a place like this?*

It was sunset when I passed through the sandstone arch and approached the final switchback. Now that it was nearly over, I felt a little sad. In the canyon I had found an awareness of myself and God that I had never known in all my seventy-six years. And surprisingly, I found it in the pain and hardship of the adventure, as well as in the grandeur and solitude of the canyon. I was leaving a friend.

As I neared the end of the trail the heavens blazed with a show of brilliant sunset colors only the western skies can produce—a farewell from the colorful canyon.

Hikers passing me on the trail had alerted everyone on top that I was coming out. The greatest moment of all, washing away all the pains and trials, was about to occur. Before me were gathered hundreds of people—strangers—who had come to see "that crazy seventy-six-year-old grandmother" climb out of the canyon. I felt a once-in-a-lifetime exhilaration.

A path opened for me and I started my victory walk through the crowd like a conquering hero. A few patted me on the shoulders, others sang out congratulations, but most stood silent, just staring at me in utter amazement as if I were a visitor from outer space. I felt twenty feet tall! It was the crowning moment of my seventy-six years.

When I reached the family and the car, my daughter was in tears—happy ones. I could see that there was both a little awe and pride in my granddaughters' expressions. Then the crowd exploded spontaneously with "Three cheers for Grandma!" Happiness was accomplishing Mission Impossible!

Frank L. Hicks, Jr.

Frank L. Hicks, Jr. wrote for popular magazines during the second half of the twentieth century.

THE HEART'S BEGINNING

Pearl S. Buck

Like it or not, life eventually comes full circle: from dependency to dependency. Mary Lou wondered why her mother was not happy about Grandfather's coming to live with them. Then she overheard a discussion having to do with Grandfather's health.

What was she to do? What could she do?

When Mary Lou came home from school she found her father doing something new. He had put a big piece of white paper on the kitchen table and he was drawing lines on it with a ruler and a black pencil. Mary Lou had skipped into the kitchen to get an apple and found her father there.

"Where's Mother?" she asked first of all.

"She's getting Timmie up from his nap," her father said, frowning at the white paper.

"What are you doing?" she asked next, but after she had taken a rather large bite of apple.

Her father pursed his lips. "I am going to build something."

"A playhouse?" She was always wanting a playhouse and since her father was a carpenter, it would be easy for him to make one for her.

"That comes next," her father said.

"Then what *are* you doing?" she asked again. Sometimes her father made her impatient because he was such a terrible tease.

"I am going to build a room onto our house," her father said softly.

"For me?" she asked.

Her father looked at her then and made a funny face. "Can't you think of somebody else?"

"But who else?" Mary Lou asked. "Oh Daddy, please tell me! Don't just be funny."

"Well," her father said, "your grandfather is coming to live with us."

This was such news that Mary Lou took three bites of apple before she asked another question. "You mean my grandfather from Kansas?"

"The same," her father said. He leaned over the paper and drew a line very carefully.

"Why is he coming to live with us?" Mary Lou asked.

"Well, he's getting old and he needs us."

"It's a long way, isn't it?" Mary Lou asked.

It was such a long way that she had never even seen her grandfather, because she lived in Pennsylvania.

"When is he coming?" Mary Lou asked.

"When your summer vacation begins," her father said.

"That," Mary Lou said, "is two whole months away."

She leaned over the paper on the table, where her father had drawn a big square and a little square.

"Bedroom," her father pointed out, "and bathroom. Nice, isn't it?"

"Why can't he sleep in the room with Timmie?" Mary Lou asked.

"He needs a room to himself," her father said, "and so does Timmie."

Mary Lou felt that she had to think things over and so she skipped away to find her mother, who was still upstairs with Timmie. Her mother was sitting in the rocking chair holding him and rocking back and forth. But she wasn't smiling.

"I was wondering where you were," she said when she saw Mary Lou.

"I was downstairs talking to Daddy," Mary Lou said. "Mother, Grandfather is coming to live with us. Isn't that wonderful?"

"I hope he will be happy here," her mother said.

"Why wouldn't he be happy?" Mary Lou asked.

"Well, he's old," her mother said.

"Very old?"

"Yes, very old."

"Fifty?" Mary Lou guessed.

"That's not old," her mother said. "At least not very old."

"Sixty?"

"Older than that."

"Whew!" Mary Lou whistled. "Seventy!"

"And more," her mother said, "but you mustn't ask him how old he is."

"Why not?"

"Because it's not polite."

"Why isn't it polite?" Mary Lou asked. "I like people to ask me how old I am."

"You won't when you get older."

"But why not, Mother?" Mary Lou asked.

Her mother suddenly got a little cross. "Oh, I don't know, Mary Lou. I wish you wouldn't keep asking questions."

Mary Lou knew her mother was not really a cross woman and when she was cross, it was because something had happened that she did not like and it was better not to ask her what it was. So Mary Lou said, "I will take Timmie outside for you, Mother. It's nice and warm."

"Thank you," her mother said. "That would be a real help."

Mary Lou asked no more questions for that day and she put Timmie's coat and cap on, which she could do very well because she was already eight years old and in the third grade, and then she took him outdoors into the yard to play in the sand pile.

When Grandfather came she could ask him all the questions she wanted to, except of course how old he was.

Every day it was exciting to see how much of the new room her father had made. Every day as soon as he came home from his job he worked on the new room and soon it began to look very nice. When the floor was done and the walls papered, Mary Lou's mother put down a green rug and at the windows she hung some green and white curtains.

"It's a nice room," Mary Lou's father said proudly.

"I hope Grandfather appreciates it," her mother said, and she was not smiling again.

Mary Lou waited until her mother had gone into the kitchen for something and then she asked her father, "Daddy, why isn't Mother happy about Grandfather's coming to live with us?"

"She's afraid she won't be able to take good enough care of him," her father said.

"But I'll help her, the way I do with Timmie," Mary Lou said.

"Good girl," her father told her. "You do that and everything will be all right."

This made her so happy that she could not keep from telling her mother that night when she was being tucked into bed.

"Mother," she said, "I am going to help you take care of Grandfather when he comes here to live."

But still her mother did not smile. "You had better wait and see how he likes children."

Mary Lou was surprised. "Why wouldn't he like children?" she asked.

"Sometimes old people don't," her mother said.

"Why don't—" Mary Lou began.

Her mother did not let her finish. "Go to sleep," she said. "It's late."

So there was another question not answered.

Oh, well, Mary Lou told herself, *when Grandfather comes I'll ask him that one too.*

When Grandfather finally came, there were quite a lot of questions that Mary Lou had saved up, but of course she could not ask them all at once. She had to wait until she knew him. They went to the station to meet him and soon the train came rushing in. Doors opened, steps were let down and people began pouring out.

Toward the back of the train, an old gentleman, very tall and thin, with white hair and a white beard, was getting down from the train. He carried a cane to help him. Mary Lou heard her father shout loudly: "Father, here we are!"

It made her feel queer for a moment to hear her father call somebody else "Father." She felt mixed-up. Suddenly, for the first time, she understood that her father had once been a little boy. She knew it, of course, for he had told her stories about living in Kansas, but it always seemed to be another boy he was talking about. Now she knew it was really he, because here was his own father, this old, old man.

"Well, Son," Grandfather said in a quiet sort of voice, "it's nice to see you." He stood leaning on his cane while they all came to shake hands with him. "And this," he said, "is Mary Lou and this is Timmie."

Grandfather was speaking their names in a low voice. Then he turned to their mother and smiled. "Marian, my dear, it's very good of you to let an old man share your home."

"You're welcome, I'm sure, Father," she said.

They got in the car and Grandfather did not say anything more. At last they were home and Mary Lou's father got out of the car first and took Grandfather's suitcase to the new room. They all went to the new room with Grandfather to see how he liked it.

"It's not quite finished," Mary Lou's father said. "I want to put in some bookcases."

"I hope you like the rug," her mother said.

"It's very nice," Grandfather said. "Very nice, indeed. I thank you all."

"Then why don't you smile?" Mary Lou asked.

"Mary Lou!" her mother cried. "You shouldn't ask such questions."

"That's all right," Grandfather said. "Children have to ask questions because it's the way they learn. I'll be smiling when I catch my breath, Mary Lou."

"We'd better let Grandfather rest," Mary Lou's mother said, and she took the children away with her and Grandfather shut the door.

"Why does he shut the door?" Mary Lou asked.

"Old people like to be quiet," her mother said.

"All the time?" Mary Lou asked. She was quite astonished because the one thing she did not like was to be quiet.

"I'm afraid so," her mother said. "But no more questions!"

There was something very different about the house now that Grandfather had come to live with the family. Mary Lou felt happier than she had ever been before but she did not know exactly why. Sometimes Grandfather was quite a lot of trouble. He had aches and pains in his bones and then he could not walk very well and there were even days when he had to stay in bed and Mary Lou's mother had to take his meals into his room on a tray. This made her a little cross again.

"Mother," Mary Lou asked her mother one morning when

they were having breakfast together and Grandfather could not get up, "do you wish that Grandfather hadn't come here?"

"Mercy, no," her mother said. "It's just that I am too busy."

"We'll all help you more," Mary Lou's father said.

"Then I needn't be cross," her mother said and smiled quite nicely.

"May I take the tray to Grandfather?" Mary Lou asked, getting up. She carried the tray carefully and when she went in, there he sat up in his bed, looking very nice and clean, his hair brushed and even his beard brushed.

"Here is your breakfast, Grandfather." Mary Lou put the tray on the table by his bed.

"Thank you, my dear," he said. "I wish I could use my legs instead of yours but this morning they decided not to work."

"Why?" Mary Lou asked. One nice thing about having Grandfather in the house was that he always had time to talk. There ought to be one grown-up in every house who has plenty of time to talk and especially to answer questions.

"Well, my legs have walked me around for a very long time," Grandfather said. "I suppose we can't blame them if they feel tired now. They do their best."

"Will my legs ever feel that way?" Mary Lou asked.

"Certainly," Grandfather said cheerfully. "But don't bother about it now. Just you run and have a good time."

There were other days when Grandfather's legs felt better and then he liked to walk with Mary Lou. On such days he joked. He said, "I really have three legs, for I think I should count my cane, don't you?"

Mary Lou laughed. "But that is a wooden leg, Grandfather!"

"All the better," Grandfather said. "It doesn't get tired."

Mary Lou felt warm and quiet and happy when she talked with Grandfather. Especially since they never had to hurry. Even walking with Grandfather was quiet and happy. If she felt like running she ran ahead and then came dancing back to him.

"I do like to see you run," Grandfather said one day. "It's a pretty sight."

Mary Lou thought of something. "Does it make you feel sorry that you can't run, Grandfather?"

"Oh, no," Grandfather said. "I have run many miles in my time. When I was your age I ran everywhere I went. I had my turn at running. This is your turn. And when you're old like me, it will be other children's turn."

Mary Lou stopped. Here was something she had never thought of before. "Will I be old like you, Grandfather?"

"I hope so," Grandfather said.

"But, Grandfather!" Mary Lou cried. It suddenly seemed frightening to think that she must one day be old and stay in bed whole days because her legs ached. Oh, and her pretty brown hair would grow white, and her smooth skin would be wrinkled like Grandfather's!

"You won't mind," Grandfather said. "It will be natural. The years slip along just as day and night slip along now and you hardly notice it, do you?"

"No," Mary Lou said solemnly. Then that was what *time* meant, something that just slipped along. "And then you die, Grandfather?"

"Well, yes and no," Grandfather said.

While they walked they had come to the edge of a field and there was a big beech tree. Mary Lou knew it very well because in summer the children on her street would play in the shade there. It was a very old tree, more than two hundred years old, her father said, and the top was dying.

"Look at the old beech," Grandfather said, pointing at it with his cane. "What do you see, Mary Lou?"

"Just an old, old tree."

"Is that all?" he asked.

She looked again. "That's all. And some little switches of trees growing around it."

"It's those little trees I see," Grandfather said. "Do you know where they come from?"

"Just wild, Grandfather."

"No," he said. "They come from the beech. That old tree knows that its time is about over and so what does it do? It tells its roots to send up a lot of little new trees. At first the new trees drink in the earth water from the old tree's roots and then they start roots of their own. By the time the old tree dies they don't need it any more. They have their own life. Still, if it hadn't been for the old tree, they wouldn't be alive. So the old tree keeps on living in them."

Mary Lou knew that Grandfather wanted her to understand something.

"You mean you are like the old tree?"

"I am, Mary Lou," he said.

"And Daddy is the new tree—and Mother?"

"And you and Timmie," he said. "It's the way life goes. You see, it never stops."

They stood for a moment looking at the great old beech. Then Mary Lou remembered a question she had forgotten to ask.

"Grandfather, you love children, don't you?"

"I do," he said. "I love them very much."

"I can feel it," Mary Lou said and she put her hand into his.

Then Grandfather said, "That's enough for one day, Mary Lou. We've been thinking big thoughts."

They walked home again and when they got there, Grandfather went to his room to rest and Mary Lou skipped out to play. She felt happy because it was interesting to talk to Grandfather and she was beginning to love him very much too.

But that same night after supper she heard a strange conversation between her mother and father! She was up in her room getting ready for bed. Timmie was already asleep and so was Grandfather. He always went to bed right after supper, the way Timmie did. But it was a beautiful warm night and Mary Lou found it hard to go to bed, and after her bath she leaned out of her window. It was just above the porch and on the porch her father and mother were sitting and talking. Mary Lou did not mean to listen but she could not help hearing what her mother suddenly said.

"Donald," her mother said, "I really think we should consider putting your father into a nursing home. He is getting too feeble."

Her father did not answer for a while. Then he said in a queer voice, "Whatever you say, Marian. I know the burden falls on you."

"It's not that," her mother said. "It's that I don't think it's good for the children to have an old person in the house. He is failing and it will make them sad. Besides, I have to tell them to be quiet in the mornings when he's asleep, and when he is sick they'll have to keep quiet all day, and that's hard on them. After all, it's their home, not his."

Her father said in the same queer voice, "Whatever you say, Marian."

For a minute Mary Lou could not believe it. Send Grandfather away just when she was beginning to love him? Oh no! She crept into bed and lay on her back, her arms under her head, and she could not sleep. Who would have time to talk with her and answer her questions if Grandfather went away? Why, Grandfather was hers and Timmie's, and how could Daddy and Mother send him away? Tears came into her eyes. How could they believe that he made Timmie and her sad? Maybe it was because Grandfather spilled things and Mother had to wash more shirts and table mats. Once when he had breakfast in bed he upset his whole tray and the sheets had to be changed. Maybe Mother was tired.

Then I'll take care of him, Mary Lou thought. *I'll tell him to hide his clothes if he spills on them and when I come home from school I'll wash them in his bathroom.*

She could not go to sleep for thinking, and when at last she did sleep it was not for all night. Her trouble woke her up in the middle of the night. Everybody was in bed now and the house was still. She got up and went to the window. The moonlight was shining down, not brightly, for the moon was low—an old moon, her father said, and it was slipping down behind the hills, beyond the field where the great beech stood.

Suddenly a light shone out of a window downstairs. It was in Grandfather's room. Then he was awake too. It would be a good time to tell him that she was going to wash his things. She tiptoed down the stairs and knocked softly on his door.

"Come in," Grandfather said.

He was sitting up against his pillows reading a book. She shut the door behind her.

"Grandfather," she said, "we must talk softly so nobody can hear us. We have to keep it a secret. I am going to wash your clothes now if you spill anything on them."

Grandfather looked astonished.

She had to tell him then what she had heard her mother say on the porch. "It isn't that Mother doesn't want you here," she said. "It's just that she is too busy and she thinks you would be more comfortable in the nursing home."

"I see," Grandfather said in a low voice.

"But I don't want you to go," Mary Lou said. She was quite surprised to find that suddenly she had to cry and she began to sob. "I like you to live here, Grandfather—it makes me feel better—"

"Thank you, dear," Grandfather said in the same low voice. "And it is sweet of you to want to wash my things, Mary Lou. But I think maybe your mother is right. I may live a long time yet and some day you would find it troublesome too to wash my things and that would make me feel badly. Don't cry, dear."

"But the little trees like to stay with the old beech," she sobbed. "They don't send it away."

"Hush, my child," he said. "Trees are not human beings."

She was kneeling by the bed now and he stroked her hair. "It's time for you to be asleep," he said.

"Aren't you going to sleep, Grandfather?"

"Old people don't need to sleep so long," he said. "Good night, Mary Lou, and don't you worry about me. Wherever I am you can come and see me."

"You shan't go," she said. "I won't let you."

"Thank you, dear child, for wanting me to stay," Grandfather said. "And good night again."

The next day when she came home from school, her father was bringing Grandfather's trunk down from the attic. Mary Lou stopped where she was just inside the door and dropped her books on the floor. "Grandfather is *not* going," she said in a loud voice.

"How did you know, Mary Lou?" her father asked, much surprised.

"I say he shan't go," she said and stamped her foot.

Her mother heard the noise and came out of the kitchen. "But Grandfather wants to go," she said. "This morning after you went to school he told us that he would be happier if he went to a good nursing home, not too far away so that you could come and see him."

"No," Mary Lou said, beginning to cry. "No, no, no!"

"Why, Mary Lou!" her mother said.

"The child is upset," her father said. "Come here, Mary Lou. What's the matter?"

They sat down on the bottom step of the stair and she cried on his shoulder.

"Now then," her father said, patting her back, "what's it all about?"

Mary Lou told him everything then.

"I heard you," she said. "I heard you talking last night. It's not true about Timmie and me being sad. I like Grandfather to be here. He is so interesting. And he isn't busy all the time. And he explained about the big beech and the little trees."

"What is the child talking about?" her mother said. "The big beech?"

"You come with me," Mary Lou said, crying very hard indeed. "Come see the big beech and I'll tell you what Grandfather explained—"

There was nothing for it except to go with her. Timmie was playing in Grandfather's room where it was quiet and he could make a house with his blocks that he kept under Grandfather's bed, and Mary Lou and her father and mother went down the road to the field where the old beech stood, sheltering the little ones.

"There it is," Mary Lou said. "Grandfather is just like that beech. He's old too but he's ours. We're the new trees, don't you see, growing out of his roots."

"Roots?" her mother said, not understanding at all.

"Oh, Mother," Mary Lou said impatiently. "I know Grandfather isn't really a tree but he's something like it. Can't you feel how Grandfather is like the old beech? And how you and Daddy and Timmie and I are the new trees? You have to feel it—I can, can't you?"

"I can," her father said gently. "I feel exactly what you mean, Mary Lou."

But her mother said nothing.

"Those little trees will grow old some day, too—Grandfather said they would," Mary Lou went on. "There will be other new trees then."

Still her mother said nothing.

"Mother," Mary Lou said, "would you like it if some day Timmie and I sent you away? When you are old?"

"No," her mother said thoughtfully, "no, I wouldn't like that."

"Oh, Mother," Mary Lou said, "now you know how I feel about Grandfather! Please don't let's send him away. I'll wash his things, I'll sweep his room. But I want to keep him because he's ours."

"Well," her mother said, "this is all very strange."

"There is a good deal in what Mary Lou is trying to tell us, Marian," her father said.

"If that's the way she feels," her mother said, "then I was completely wrong last night."

"Thank you, my dear," he said. "We'll all be happier, I think."

So that was the way it ended. They walked home together and as soon as they got there Mary Lou's father took the trunk upstairs again. Then they went into Grandfather's room. Timmie was putting a steeple on a church he had built while they were away and Grandfather was sitting in the rocking chair watching him. On the bed were some neat piles of clothes he had got ready to put in the trunk.

"You may as well put those clothes away again, Father," Mary Lou's father said. "We have decided that we can't spare you. You'll just have to stay with us."

Grandfather looked up surprised. "But I thought—" he began.

"No buts, Grandfather," Mary Lou's mother said in a nice bright voice. "Mary Lou took us down to the big beech tree and explained how she felt."

"Oh, Grandfather," Mary Lou said, "please, please, stay with us."

Grandfather's cheeks were suddenly pink above his white beard. "Well," he said, "well, well, well—if that's the way you feel—"

"Oh, I do," Mary Lou said.

"Then so do I," Grandfather said.

Pearl S. Buck
(1892–1973)

Pearl S. Buck towers over twentieth-century American literature, being one of those rare few who were awarded both the Pulitzer Prize and the Nobel Prize for Literature. Born in Hillsboro, West Virginia, she spent much of her early life in China. Her best-sellers include *The Good Earth* (1931) and *Dragon Seed* (1942).

BREAD CRUSTS

Louise Seymour Hasbrouck

"You're getting more like your Great-aunt Beulah every day," said Grandpa to Rita. She quickly realized the resemblance was anything but a compliment.

But at least she was better than Peggy!

Or . . . was she?

"If you don't look out, Mary, you'll spoil Rita," commented Grandfather Wainwright.

"Spoil *Rita?"* queried Mrs. Wainwright, turning, surprised, with her hand on the doorknob. She was going to her evening session at the library. "You mean Peggy, don't you? I suppose we do spoil her, but she does love parties so, and Rita is just naturally a stay-at-home, and so unselfish!" It was so much of a common occurrence in the Wainwright household that somebody must stay home with Grandfather on account of his weak heart that even Grandfather himself had ceased to protest about it.

"I don't mean Peggy, I mean Rita!" insisted old Mr. Wainwright.

Mrs. Wainwright regarded him with astonished eyes as she buttoned her coat. Then her expression changed. One could not expect Father to always keep his own keen mind.

"I'll try not to spoil either of them," she assured him, slipping through the living room to speak to Rita, who was washing the supper dishes in the kitchen.

"You'll remember, dear, to give Grandpa his medicine at 8:30, won't you?" she queried.

"Of course I will, Mother," answered Rita, a tall, pale, and conscientious-looking girl.

"My dear, thoughtful, unselfish daughter!" whispered Mrs. Wainwright, with a little hug.

Rita's face colored faintly and she tried not to look self-satisfied. Praise like this, especially from her mother, whom she adored, was very sweet to her.

"After I play dominoes with Grandfather, I'll mend that dress of Peggy's," she promised. "She never will do it herself, you know."

"It would be so nice if you would!"

Mrs. Wainwright departed. Peggy, sixteen, pretty and curly haired, tripped downstairs and demanded of her grandfather, "How do you like me, Grandpa, in my new apricot?"

"You'll pass[3] any place where they're not too particular. Kind of a pity your hair and skirts don't keep up with the rest of you, though."

"Grandpa, you certainly put a mean twist in your compliments. You wouldn't want me to be a back number[4], would you?"

His reply was cut short by Rita, who appeared from the dining room where she had been putting away dishes, saying, "Do keep still a minute, Peggy! Something is wrong here!"

A shade came over Peggy's face as she surveyed Rita on her knees, busy about her skirt. It was not her night to do the supper dishes, but nevertheless, the sight of the pile of unwashed supper dishes through the open door gave her a guilty pang.

"Oh, Rita, it seems mean for me to be going out all the time instead of you. I'll finish the dishes for you, and I wish you'd go in my place tonight."

"Yes, this is a fine time to say it!" scoffed Rita, rising. Like many self-denying persons, she was somewhat given to remarks with prickles in them.

"But I did say so when we were first invited!" Peggy protested.

"Did you?"

Rita's indulgent tone did not make the younger sister any more comfortable, nor did her little superior smile.

After Peggy had gone, Rita fetched the dominoes with a discontented face, for after all, she was a young girl, and human.

"Play a game, Grandfather?"

[3] *Pass inspection.*
[4] *Behind the times.*

"If you want to," replied Grandfather, and it suddenly struck Rita that he said it just as though he were humoring her.

"Why, I don't care about it," she was irritated into admitting. "I only play on your account!"

"It's just as I said," remarked Grandfather dreamily. "Your mother and Peggy are spoiling you. You're getting more like your Great-aunt Beulah every day!"

"Spoiling me? What do you mean?" demanded the astounded Rita.

"She was the most unpleasantly unselfish person I ever knew!" reminisced Grandfather further.

"Grandfather!"

"Yes, ma'am—too unselfish to live, or rather, to live with! She drove us all crazy. You couldn't be comfortable a minute when she was in the room; she was always bothering you to move nearer the light or out of the draft or something—and you couldn't get a crust of bread when she was at the table!"

"But did the other people want the crusts?" inquired Rita dazedly.

"No, but they'd have liked a chance to be unselfish, too. Most everybody would." Here Grandfather took up his paper and calmly began reading.

After a moment of flushed, indignant silence, Rita went to find Peggy's torn dress. Very well! If Grandfather didn't appreciate her, Mother did! And others, too! Peggy might be the prettier, the more popular sister, but had she not overheard two of Peggy's very best friends, when discussing who would be present at the festivity, say one to the other:

"Rita Wainwright won't go, of course! She always stays home with her grandfather and lets Peggy have the good times. Rita has a wonderful character, you know—so unselfish!"

Peggy thoroughly enjoyed the party. She always did. But it seemed that there was something still more gorgeous on foot, a seashore picnic! "You've got to come along, Rita," she insisted the next day at dinner. "Mother will be home from the library tomorrow, you know."

"But we haven't any bathing suits!" The Wainwrights had only lived in this seaside town for a few months since their widowed mother had obtained the position of librarian, and had hardly had time or money to acquire such extras.

"Mildred is sure she can borrow some for us. That's probably her phoning now." Peggy ran to the telephone, and came back in a moment looking very much disappointed.

"Mildred says everybody on earth seems to be planning to use bathing suits on this holiday, so all she can borrow is one."

"Then you'll go, of course!" said Rita.

"I don't see why! You learned to swim, you know, on your visit to Grandfather's before we came here, and I never have. Anyway, it's your turn; oh, more than your turn. Please do go!"

But deep down in Rita's heart there was a qualm at the idea of going off with the "crowd," Peggy's crowd, she considered them, though several of the boys and girls were her own age. She was so quiet and not pretty! They wouldn't like her as they did Peggy. But now—well, they admired her anyway, and that was something. Looking up, she met her mother's softly expectant gaze.

"Of course I wouldn't deprive you of the pleasure!" she said, in her most elder-sister manner.

"Bread crusts!" murmured Grandfather Wainwright, with a mischievous smile over his plate.

Rita grew hot all over.

"Is the bread baked too hard, Father?" inquired Mrs. Wainwright, innocently. "I should have made biscuits for you, but—"

"Don't make them for me!" said Grandfather. "Rita might like a crusty one now and then."

Rita pushed away her plate. If Grandfather kept this up, she would leave the table. Peggy looked from one to the other wonderingly. Then the clock chimed.

"There, it's three!" said Peggy. "I promised to go with Harriet and play hymns for the children at the orphanage. It's such a lark! They love it, and you ought to hear them sing, the poor dears! 'Scuse me, please, Mother and 'scuse me, please, if I grab your dishes and deprive any one of a last bite. They've got to be done in just five minutes." And in just five minutes she dashed off on her mission, which in some girls might have seemed unselfish, but to Peggy was apparently only more fun.

Next morning the sun rose in all its splendor, ushering in a perfect picnic day. Mildred arrived at the Wainwrights's with her one borrowed bathing suit.

Peggy, who opened the door, welcomed her.

"You're going, aren't you, Peggy?" inquired Mrs. Wainwright placidly. "I thought, when it came to the point, Rita wouldn't let you stay home."

"Why, I really don't know. I'll ask her again." Peggy called to Rita above. "Oh, Rita. Here's Mildred. Are you going or not?"

Rita descended deliberately. "I told you I wouldn't," she began, when Grandfather looked meaningfully at her from his corner. He formed two words with his lips.

"Perhaps I will go. After all, it is my turn," she suddenly replied.

"Why, that's fine!" Peggy stammered, making a heroic effort to hide her surprise.. Mildred, a blunt youngster, stared at Rita, amazed and disappointed.

"Oh, I thought of course Peggy would go!" she exclaimed.

Worse than anything for Rita was her mother's surprised face. Yet she bravely kept to her decision.

"Peggy has been telling me I ought to accept invitations more," she explained to Mildred; then, without waiting for the latter's lame rejoinder, she sped back upstairs, hearing, as she went, Peggy remark indignantly to her friend, "Mildred, you've as much tact as—as a can opener! And Rita is a regular dear—"

With tears in her eyes, Rita dressed. She would try to be frivolous now! She would go on the picnic even if Mother did call Peggy her unselfish daughter!

Late that afternoon a sunburned quartet noisily entered the Wainwright house. It was Mildred, her brother Harry, his friend Stanley Richards, and Rita. But not the same Rita who had gone out that morning. Here was a pink-cheeked, bright-eyed girl, positively handsome!

"Just stopped in to tell you how we missed you, Peggy!" cried Mildred for the crowd. "But we must tell you that your sister is a good sport, too! And a wonder in the water. And as for boiling cocoa and frying eggs over a driftwood fire and leading the singing, she simply can't be beat!"

Peggy beamed at the assembled boys and girls.

"Glad you waked up!" she said. "Didn't I say you didn't realize the abilities of my distinguished sister?"

Rita felt all washed, inside and out, with fresh air and happy thoughts. How unkind she had been about Peggy! Putting her in a false position so often just that she herself might feel superior.

"Strikes me you haven't been moping yourself, Peggy," observed Stanley. "Who'd you make all this fudge and popcorn for? Us weary swimmers?"

"I should say not!" cried Peggy. "Though you're welcome to the leftovers. I had the time of my life. Walter Eaton, the lame boy, you know, from across the street, and his sister, Marie, and I had a party. I just love to stay at home. It's a circus!"

"Grandfather," cried Rita, "she likes bread crusts, too!"

"Of course she does! She spells her name P-e-g, not P-i-g!" replied her shrewd ancestor.

"Tell me, what is this code you and Grandfather are always talking?" inquired Peggy.

"Some other time. They'll eat all that popcorn before I get a bit if I explain it to you now!" replied her reformed sister.

Louise Seymour Hasbrouck
(1883–?)

Louise Seymour Hasbrouck wrote for inspirational and popular magazines during the first half of the twentieth century. She was born in Ogdensburg, New York. Among her published books are *LaSalle* (1916), *Israel Putnam* (1916), and *Those Careless Kincaids* (1928).

HIS FIRST DRESS SUIT

Felicia Buttz Clark

College was new to Harry, and he so much wanted to be accepted by Otis, the son of a wealthy steel man and the campus trendsetter. Before long, Harry was in over his head financially. How could he get out of this? What would Grandpa have done in his place?

Harry Harper was visiting his grandfather's beautiful old farmhouse in New York state. Strange to say, it was the first time that he had seen his grandparents since he was a little boy, because his father's home was in far-away California, and there had never been money enough under the rose-covered roof of the bungalow by the seashore to take anyone but Mother on that long and expensive journey east.

And now Harry was nineteen and just entering college. While appreciative of the western institutions, both Mr. and Mrs. Harper desired Harry to go to the college where his father had been educated.

Harry's father had never been very successful financially, so Harry could have little help from home, and must earn most of what he required to pay for board and books and fun. It seemed an easy task to contemplate, when one was under the sheltering roof of home; it grew more perplexing as the train swept on and on across the mountains and prairies, and into the more populous regions.

At Chicago, a youth boarded the train who, on seeing Harry, began to be friendly. It turned out that his goal was the same as that of the lad from California.

"Going to Amherst, eh?" he asked. "Well, I'm bound there myself. Fine old place. Jolly fellows. You'll have a good time."

"It was my father's college," remarked Harry, with that pride in his tone that always made it sound affectionate when he spoke of his father.

"What's his name?"

"Henry L. Harper. I'm the junior Henry."

Harry felt sure that everyone who knew Amherst would know his father's name.

"Never heard of him. My father is Samuel Perkins.

Incidentally, he's a steel man, and gave a hundred thousand dollars for the new gym."

"Oh!" replied Harry, and withdrew into his shell of reserve.

He soon came out of it, for Otis Perkins became very companionable, took Harry into the dining car, and insisted on paying for the dinner.

"Aw, what's the use of making a fuss over a little thing like that," he insisted. "Some fellows have more cash than others, that's all, and I'm one of the lucky ones."

There was a bit of condescension in this remark which did not penetrate to Harry's brain. It was kind of Otis, and he appreciated it. By the time they reached Pittsburgh, where their ways parted, the two lads were good friends, and though Otis was a junior and Harry was a freshman, they pledged their word to each other that this class difference should not part them.

"When you get to college, I must take you to my tailor," suggested Otis, with an appraising glance at Harry's brown suit.

"I can't buy any more clothes." Harry's face flushed.

"O, that's all right, of course, but it makes you look a bit peculiar. I didn't mean anything, old chap. Good-by! We'll meet later."

Otis waved his hand and picked up a handsome leather suitcase that made Harry's old one, used by his mother on her occasional trips to the East, look worn and shabby.

As the train sped through fertile valleys and past serene lakes bordered by comfortable homes, into the heart of New York state, Harry felt suddenly timid and lonely. The brown suit was new. Mother was sure that it would last two years, at least, with the help of another pair of trousers. That was in the trunk.

Grandfather's house was in this lovely farmland, making a garden spot of the center of New York state, and Grandfather himself, silvery hair floating in the soft breeze, his wrinkled face bright with smiles, was at the station to meet Harry, with his modest little car.

"We'll have some good rides around the country, my boy," the old man said, after he had asked about all the family. "My sakes, Harry, when I saw you last, you were the most mischievous ever. We had great times together. Remember the snail? Never saw such a big one in all my days! Don't have them in this part of the old United States. But we have things just as good. I caught a turtle the other day with 1720 stamped on his back. Ever hear of that out in California? But I keep forgetting that you're going to college, and here I am talking to a learned chap like you about snails and turtles, when I ought to be saying things in Greek and Latin. That's the kind of talk you fellows are used to, isn't it?"

"Well, I guess not, Grandpa," Harry replied, and they laughed together.

They rushed by the orchards where apples hung red upon the trees, past white churches and small villages, for Grandfather enjoyed driving fast, and Harry thought of Otis Perkins, whose chief object in life seemed to be dinners and clothes. Evidently it was old-fashioned to go to college to study. According to Otis, college life seemed to be one grand rush of football games, dances, and larks.

"Here we are. There's Grandma. Well, I've brought the boy, Lizzie, and for the life of me, I can't make out whether he looks most like Henry or Elizabeth."

It was good to be in Grandfather's house, so homey and pleasant with its broad porch and white pillars, its garden full of purple and white asters, its low-ceilinged rooms and open fireplace where a log was ablaze. College, and Otis, and the strange future no longer filled Harry's mind. He ate cottage cheese and gingersnaps, and told the dear old folks all about California and his life there, about the lilies that whiten the fields by the thousands, and the gorgeous geraniums with scarlet and pink blooms that make unsightly places beautiful.

"Time to go to bed," Grandma said, when the tall clock with the moon face struck nine.

Harry arose to say good night when, to his surprise, he saw his grandfather take a well-worn Bible from a shelf.

Henry Harper, Harry's father, was a Christian man. His family went regularly to church, they supported all benevolences, so far as their means permitted, and no meal was eaten without seeking God's blessing, but they never had family worship. Perhaps it may seem strange, but it is true that Harry Harper, although educated in the Sunday school and properly brought up at home, had never before been in a home where family prayers were held.

He sat down and waited, watching the light upon the old man's white hair, watching his grandmother as she placidly rocked back and forth in her high-backed chair. It was so restful in that living-room of the old house, so far removed from the world and its bustle, the money-making world, where men jostled each other in a mad quest for the gold that perishes.

"The Lord is my light and my salvation; whom shall I fear? the Lord is the strength of my life; of whom shall I be afraid?" Grandfather read. He scarcely seemed to look at the text because he knew the words so well. He and Grandma had read from this old book every morning and evening for fifty years. Their minds were full of the quaint expressions of the old King James edition.

Harry saw the log break into flame, burst open, and fall to glowing ashes as he listened. The psalm he had heard before, but never had its beauty so impressed him.

"Hear, O Lord, when I cry with my voice: have mercy also upon me, and answer me. . . . Hide not thy face far from me; . . . thou hast been my help; leave me not, neither forsake me, O God of my salvation. When my father and mother forsake me, then the Lord will take me up."

A week later, Grandfather drove Harry in the little car the five miles to the station.

"Keep close to Him, Harry my boy," he said, as he looked up into the tall young man's face. "You'll meet temptation, my boy; it'll come when you least expect it, but keep close to the Savior, Harry."

Now, in college, there wasn't much time to think. Otis Perkins took Harry Harper up as a sort of protégé. He got him into his set, he showed him the town. Perkins had his own car, and they scoured the country round and went on one grand tour to Boston, where Otis paid the bills. Harry protested, but he knew very well that out of his slender funds, rapidly, O, so rapidly! diminishing, he could not afford to go to hotels.

One morning, he faced the inevitable. He had just fifty dollars left to pull him through the rest of the year, and it was only January now. No work had turned up for him to do, and he had not sought it. This made him ashamed. Why had he not tried to get some honest occupation as many others of his companions had done? Because of the association with Otis Perkins, whose father was rich enough to give one hundred thousand dollars for a gym.

Harry drummed on the windowpane and looked out at the glistening snow that clothed the campus with a spotless garment and hung the ivy vines on the gray buildings with festoons. A vision came to him of a low bungalow, where even now flowers were blooming. His mother was busy about her work. His father was bringing home a letter from Harry. There were five other children in the bungalow, and they must all have an education. One of his ambitions had been to take care of himself and help them. It was only January, and all but fifty dollars of what his father had given him was gone. To write home for more was impossible. His father did not have it to give.

He wouldn't care if it weren't for Otis Perkins, who had no idea what it meant to be poor, who spent fifty dollars and thought nothing of it! Harry was proud to be the friend of Samuel Perkins's son. And Otis himself was at heart an honest, whole-souled fellow. He had no idea that he was leading Harry to have false ideals.

"Look here, Harry," Otis called out, as he entered Harry's room, shaking a thick, white envelope at him. "Here's an invitation from Adelaide Sipher, the girl over at Smith that I told you about. There's going to be doings over there, and I'm to bring one man with me, and that's going to be you, my boy."

"But—" stammered Harry. He had meant to say: "I can't go. I haven't suitable clothes," but the words died on Harry's lips in the presence of Otis Perkins.

Life seemed very hard just at that moment. Harry had a social soul. He missed his two sisters, one two years older, the other just sixteen, and really longed to get out among the lively crowd of girls at Smith College. Otis had told him how pretty Adelaide Sipher was, and how she, too, was from California.

"O, I say, Harry, what's the matter with you this morning? If it's only a dress suit that stands in the way, why don't you go and buy one?"

Why, indeed? thought Harry, with grim humor. *Fifty dollars left for dress suit, board, fees, etc., for half a year.*

"You can go down to my tailor and get one made to order. I suppose your folks didn't know how things are here. One can't get along without extra money for entertainment."

Harry knew of several places where he could have had a very good time, if he had possessed the required clothes. It was equally true that his mother and father had not realized the necessity for such attire in modern college life. Times had changed since Henry Harper went to Amherst. Then, a Sunday suit had answered for all occasions, and a fellow was lucky to own one of them.

"You'll have to go without me, Otis." He did not turn from the window, but he no longer saw the snow nor the vision of a flower-hidden bungalow. There was a mist in front of his eyes that made him feel ashamed. For a moment Harry Harper wished heartily that he was not a student at Amherst.

"O, I say," began Otis, beginning to be embarrassed.

He had never been up against such a situation before. He had refrained from any further references to clothes from a certain delicacy of feeling because he really liked Harry; still he had felt that the brown suit that he wore required some apology, it was so far from the eastern cut as to make both of them conspicuous. But this was different. A fellow might wear old-fashioned clothes around college, but he must have a dress suit for special occasions.

"Maybe your money hasn't yet come from home?" he added with an inspiration. "Never mind a little thing like that. Come on down to Astor's. I'll have it charged to my account, and you can pay me when you get the cash. I often have to make Astor wait. He knows me, and won't say a word."

There are times when pride makes cowards out of brave men.

Looking into Otis's good-humored face, the face of a lad who had never known misfortune or sacrifice, who had had the cornucopia of fortune emptied upon him with all its treasures, Harry, inexperienced, a little overawed, with an intense desire to enjoy life and all its good things, had not the courage to say: "I am poor; I cannot pay for a new suit. I must earn my way."

When that dress suit came to his room, Harry wasn't sure whether he was glad or sorry. It was of expensive cloth, as Otis had said that it did not pay to buy cheap material; it was cut in the latest style and accompanied with all the accessories—silk vest, silk shirt, handsome cuff buttons, and white tie. Otis said that these things were necessary, and Harry, in the resignation of despair, saw the bill mounting and mounting upward toward a hundred dollars.

Well, he was in for it now, and might as well enjoy himself; so he put on the suit, and when he looked at his image in the glass, a truly handsome specimen of young manhood, he could not keep back a pleased smile. He was seeing college life under the best auspices, those of such a fellow as Otis Perkins. Surely the folks at home would want him to have a good time. And in some way he'd manage to pay for all his fun—in some way.

What a glorious evening that was!

"Now that's a smart-looking suit," said Otis. "Clothes do make a great difference in a fellow's appearance, just as they do in a girl's."

The little imp in Harry's brain whispered, *If the fellows can pay for them,* and Harry wanted to stifle that imp's voice. It stayed with him all through that truly delightful evening, when he and Adelaide, a fine-looking, dark-haired girl with laughing eyes, sat in a nook by some palms while the others made merry, and Harry told her about his home in California and she told him about hers. Somehow, before he knew it, he had told Adelaide that he must earn his way, and had not been ashamed a bit, while he would have feared to be so frank with Otis. And she had asked him what he was going to do.

He saw her looking at his stylish get-up with some curiosity, and almost . . . almost, he divulged the whole story of the suit, because she reminded him so much of his older sister, Belle. And then he remembered how freely he had been speaking to a stranger, and closed up in his usual shell of reserve.

Yes, it had been a splendid evening, so he said to Otis as the car shot out into the darkness. He leaned his head back on the cushion and thought it all over. Adelaide was a nice girl, but it came to him that she had not been very explicit about her people, when he had talked so freely about his. What had possessed him to be such an idiot! Probably because she had eyes like Belle's.

A glaring headlight, a bump, an exclamation from Otis, who pushed hard on the brakes, and Harry found himself in a ditch, unhurt but dizzy!

"Are you all right?" asked Otis. "Those people knocked us over and then went on their heartless way. I guess the car will have to stay where it is now till tomorrow, and we'll have to walk home. Lucky it isn't very far, but the snow's beginning to melt and it's raining. Haven't a raincoat or umbrella, either of us. Well, accidents will happen."

"I'm ready," said Harry, and they plunged into the gloom of a country road.

Down poured the rain. The snow had melted to a mass of slush, the few lights were hidden by mist. Stumbling, slipping, they progressed slowly, and it was two o'clock in the morning before they reached the dormitory, and parted.

"I'll see you later," called out Otis, as they staggered, almost exhausted, into the warm hall.

Then Harry went to his room, took off that dress suit, and viewed the remains. When people get to the very worst, they are usually calm. Harry was coldly calm. He felt as if he were all frozen up inside of that part of him that feels. His body was burning with the struggle and exercise of the walk, but his soul was petrified.

The suit was utterly ruined. His overcoat sleeve was torn and the undercoat sleeve also. Probably caught on a corner of the car. His entire suit was soaking wet, and his light shoes, the first pair of patent leathers that he had ever had, were ruined.

"About as good a job as rain and slush and the accident could do," observed Harry drily. "I'll go to bed."

Dawn found him still sleepless, still pondering the problem. Eighty-seven dollars due to Otis for a ruined suit; seventy-five dollars at midyear for dues, and so on and so on. The little imp in his brain delighted to add at the end of the calculation, *And how are you going to pay for it all?*

The next morning Harry got up late and looked at his face as he had done the evening before, but there wasn't any proud smile now. Grim determination was written there; the spirit of his Puritan ancestors was in the firm set of his mouth, the erect position of his head. For, in the darkness of the night, he had made the hardest resolve of his life. He would tell Otis Perkins the exact truth. Probably it would mean an end to the friendship of which he had felt so proud, for he had been keen enough to discover several traits of snobbishness in his idol.

It was hard. It sounds trivial perhaps, but for Harry Harper in his brown suit to go deliberately to Otis Perkins and say that he was poor, that he must work at anything he could find to earn money to pay for an evening suit and other things that he couldn't afford, was as hard as for a soldier to walk up to the mouth of a cannon. So hard it was that Harry began to feel it was impossible. He just couldn't do it.

He sat down limply by the window and began to rock back and forth. The rhythm of the movement reminded him of something; what was it?

Now he remembered: Grandmother had rocked placidly back and forth those nights in the living-room while Grandfather had read from the old Book. What had made the white-haired man's face so peaceful? What had made Grandmother's lips so smiling, her expression so kindly? Was it the constant hearing of words of comfort and cheer?

Harry went to the closet and took out the Bible that had always rested on his bureau at home, although he had not read it very often. Here, in college, he had been a little ashamed to have it in plain sight. None of the men in Otis Perkins's circle had any such book in view. There were plenty of illustrated papers and books, but few Bibles.

At Psalms he opened, his unaccustomed fingers searching for the place where Grandfather had read on that first night after his arrival. Family prayers, the old-fashioned kind, were so novel to him that he remembered everything distinctly.

Yes, here it was. Harry read it over, eagerly, for he was in genuine need of help. If constant communion with God through his Word had given to those old people that benign and peaceful look, would it bring comfort to him, a boy, timid before the new phases of temptation and confusion which college life had brought to him?

"The Lord is my light and my salvation; whom shall I fear? the Lord is the strength of my life; of whom shall I be afraid?"

It seemed to him that he could hear the quaver in Grandfather's voice now.

"Wait on the Lord: be of good courage, and he shall strengthen thine heart: wait, I say, on the Lord."

Harry had never felt the real beauty and comfort of these words till in this hour of need. Had an evening dress suit, a few hours of amusement in clothes that he could not possibly pay for, been worth the anxiety that they had cost him?

Otis Perkins was not in his room, his chum said. He was off for the day. That was discouraging. Harry was worked up to the pitch of making a clean breast of all his faults and failings. Now he must keep up his courage for several hours, perhaps till the next day. He could feel it slowly oozing out of him as he ran down the steps of the dormitory and walked across the campus under the splendid, drooping elm trees, bare branches stretched out against the wintry sky.

Entering his room, he threw himself down into an easy-chair, without noticing that there was a white-haired man seated in the farther corner, reading the morning newspaper.

"What's the matter, Harry?" asked a cheerful voice.

"O Grandfather!" exclaimed the lad, hugging him hard. "I'm so glad to see you!"

"Well, this welcome is flattering," replied Grandfather, his eyes twinkling. "But it strikes me that my reception is extra warm. Have you been getting into some scrape, young man, and you want your elderly relative to pull you out?"

"That's just about it, Grandpa."

Grandfather laid aside his paper.

"Tell me all about the scrape, boy, and I'll help you."

So Harry told everything. How proud he had been to have the son of so well-known a man as Samuel Perkins for his friend, and how he had tried to keep up with him and had spent almost all the money that his father had expected would "help out" during the year, supplemented with the dire disaster to the dress suit.

When, with a tragic face, he exhibited the tattered remains of what had been a handsome suit, Grandfather blew his nose energetically and coughed in an extraordinary manner. His eyes twinkled more than ever, for Grandfather had once been young himself.

"Went to see a girl, did you, and thought you had to be all dressed up to find favor in her eyes?"

"Most of the fellows had on evening suits, Grandfather," protested Harry.

"But not all."

"No."

"Probably couldn't afford it and wouldn't go in debt," commented Grandfather. "What is the girl's name?"

"Adelaide Sipher."

"O yes, old Dick Sipher's granddaughter. Lives just out here a few miles. I know him well. We'll see. Yes, we'll see. And now, Harry, how much money do you need?"

Grandfather held out a fat roll of bills.

"You—you wouldn't lend me some, would you, Grandfather?"

"Lend it to you, you young rascal? No, I'll *give* it to you. Will a hundred dollars pay what you owe to this Perkins?"

"It'll leave something over."

"All right. Now, you just settle that up, and I don't believe it's necessary to go into details with him in this matter. You've told me and relieved your mind, and from the looks of you, I think you've had a bad night."

"O Grandfather!"

"No, you needn't thank me. Why did the Lord give me such a fine grandson, if it wasn't so that I could give him a little lift when he's in trouble? And I say, you'd better not write Mother anything about this. It's a secret between ourselves."

"I'm glad to be relieved of that unpleasant task, so I'll promise you solemnly, Grandfather—"

"That you won't go into debt any more in order to shine in the eyes of the girls, eh? Well, that's all right. Adelaide Sipher would like you just as well in your brown suit as she would in the long-tailed togs, if she's anything like her grandmother. She was a fine girl. And now, Harry, let's get lunch and then go out to Dick Sipher's. He has a big dairy farm run on the latest plans, and I'll warrant that he'll have some work for you to do that wouldn't upset your dignity a bit. Like to fuss around flowers, don't you?"

"I like it best of all, Grandpa."

Harry sat close to his grandfather all the way out to Richard Sipher's. Somehow it made him feel better and stronger to be near him.

Bravely he wore his old brown suit all that year, and bravely he worked in the large greenhouses on Mr. Sipher's farm, not minding a bit when Adelaide came to her grandfather's, and found him with hands covered with loam. He and Adelaide grew to be good friends, and when Mr. Sipher invited him to a special dinner party for Adelaide, it aroused the envy of Otis Perkins, who had become somewhat cold and patronizing.

Just before commencement there came a big pasteboard box for Mr. Harry Harper. Opening it, he found a handsome evening suit. On it lay a card from Grandfather:

"For the boy who is ashamed to wear clothes that he cannot pay for and is not ashamed to work."

Felicia Buttz Clark

(1862–?)

Felicia Buttz Clark was born in New York City, and wrote during the last part of the nineteenth century and the first third of the twentieth century. Among her published books are *The Cripple of Nuremburg* (1900), *The Sword of Garibaldi* (1905), and *Laughing Water* (1915).

AMY'S BUTTERFLY

Kathryn Smith Boyette

Lovely Amy fit that terrible label—mentally handicapped. Even so, she was all the world to her grandmother.

When she was six, there came that dreadful, lonely day . . .

Amy, with her huge green eyes, looked at me and smiled. "When, Grandmom?" she asked as she pointed to the cocoon hanging from a branch of the azalea bush.

"It should happen any day now," I answered.

"What did you say it was?" she asked for the tenth time in less than an hour.

"A cocoon," I answered, and then explained how a butterfly was forming inside.

Amy lay back on the ground, satisfied with the answer, and gazed into the open spaces of the skies. I loved the company of my granddaughter. Amy's questions seemed endless. She had an innocent amazement at the world that brightened my days. In moments like this, it was hard to believe she was different.

Different. I didn't like that word. What was so different about Amy? People often used the word *special,* but that word was awkward in this situation. I looked at her face daydreaming into the clouds. Amy was my greatest blessing, but I longed for her to be normal. In days like this even my longing seemed wrong. After all, what was so abnormal about Amy?

Amy was the third child of my daughter, Bess. She was beautiful, but from the beginning she had been slower to respond than the other children. Bess and I had sensed that something was wrong, long before Amy was diagnosed as mildly retarded.

"She can be educated," the doctors said. "She will just be slower to learn."

"She will need extra help," another had commented.

Those words echoed in my mind as if a judge had handed down a life sentence. My beautiful grandchild was retarded and no matter how hard I wished otherwise, my Amy would remain retarded.

My husband had died shortly after Amy's birth. For the first time in my life I lived alone. So when Bess returned to work when Amy was three, she suggested that I baby-sit. It wasn't long before I was devoting my life to Amy.

It was after seven o'clock one evening when Bess finally came for Amy, who had eaten dinner an hour before and was sleeping soundly on the couch.

"Did you two have a nice day?" Bess asked.

"As always," I answered. "You're late."

"Did you have plans?" she asked.

"No, I just worried."

Bess smiled. "We found a school for Amy."

"School?" I responded, shocked at the idea.

"She is six now," she said, trying to calm me.

"You can't send her to school! She's different!"

"It's a special school," Bess said, and picked up Amy.

I stood at the window and cried as Bess carried the sleeping child to the car. *How could she do this?*

Bess called on Sunday, hoping my anger had cooled, but I could hardly talk to her. A lump crowded my throat and tears trickled down my cheeks. She told me that Amy got out of school at three and asked if I would pick her up. I knew she was hoping three hours a day would fill our needs. I told her I'd be there.

The day seemed long—endless, in fact. My house was empty once again. The soap operas filled the living room as I sat in front of the television, not watching. I prayed that Amy would not be hurt at school. I imagined her among children who were deformed and distorted, children who screamed and shook. Amy was not like the children I pictured. She was beautiful and fragile. Her slowness was her only problem. What she needed was love and protection, not a school for "special" children.

At three o'clock, I was sitting on the steps of Amy's school, impatiently waiting. After ten minutes, I rose to look for her. Then I saw her coming toward me with another child by the hand.

"Lisa!" she squealed with excitement. "This is Grandmom." They ran to me. "Lisa is my best friend!"

Lisa was not at all like I had pictured Amy's classmates. She was a wide-eyed, dark-haired girl, almost as beautiful as Amy. A lump grew in my throat. Amy had a friend her own age. I should be glad. Instead, I felt a sense of loss. Had Amy missed me at all?

When the girls said good-bye, Amy got in the car. As soon as we arrived home, she bounced out of the car and quickly ran over to the azalea bush in my backyard.

"There's a hole, Grandmom!" she shouted.

"What?"

"A hole," she said again as she started to cry. The hole that disturbed her was the one the moth had eaten in the cocoon. I tried to comfort her, but she knew the cocoon was empty. Then I spotted the moth a few feet away, stretched out on the grass in the sun.

"Look, Amy, there he is. Don't cry," I said, pointing.

She smiled and ran toward him. "Don't you run away! Come back, butterfly," she said as she clamped her hand around him.

"No, Amy dear, you can't keep him," I said as I gently pried open her tiny, clenched hand.

"But he's mine, Grandmom!" she said.

"No, Amy, he's God's butterfly." I understood just how Amy felt, for I knew that I had been no less selfish in holding on to *her.*

"Amy, in a little while he'll fly," I said to her.

"I don't want him to fly! He's mine!"

We sat down on the ground, and I held her close. After almost an hour of impatient waiting, we saw the moth begin to flutter its wings. Soon it flapped its wings clumsily, and then, like a kite, it rose from the ground. Amy ran to it, waving her arms.

"Butterfly!" she said and laughed as it gracefully flew from her sight.

I loosened the cocoon from the azalea bush and placed it in Amy's hand. We lay back in the grass and talked about the butterfly—and the new school. We were lying there in the near darkness when Bess came.

Amy pinned the cocoon on my living-room curtain. It served as a constant reminder. It hadn't been easy to let go of Amy. But we never doubted that she, like the butterfly forming in the cocoon, could fly too.

Kathryn Smith Boyette

Kathryn Smith Boyette wrote for popular magazines during the second half of the twentieth century.

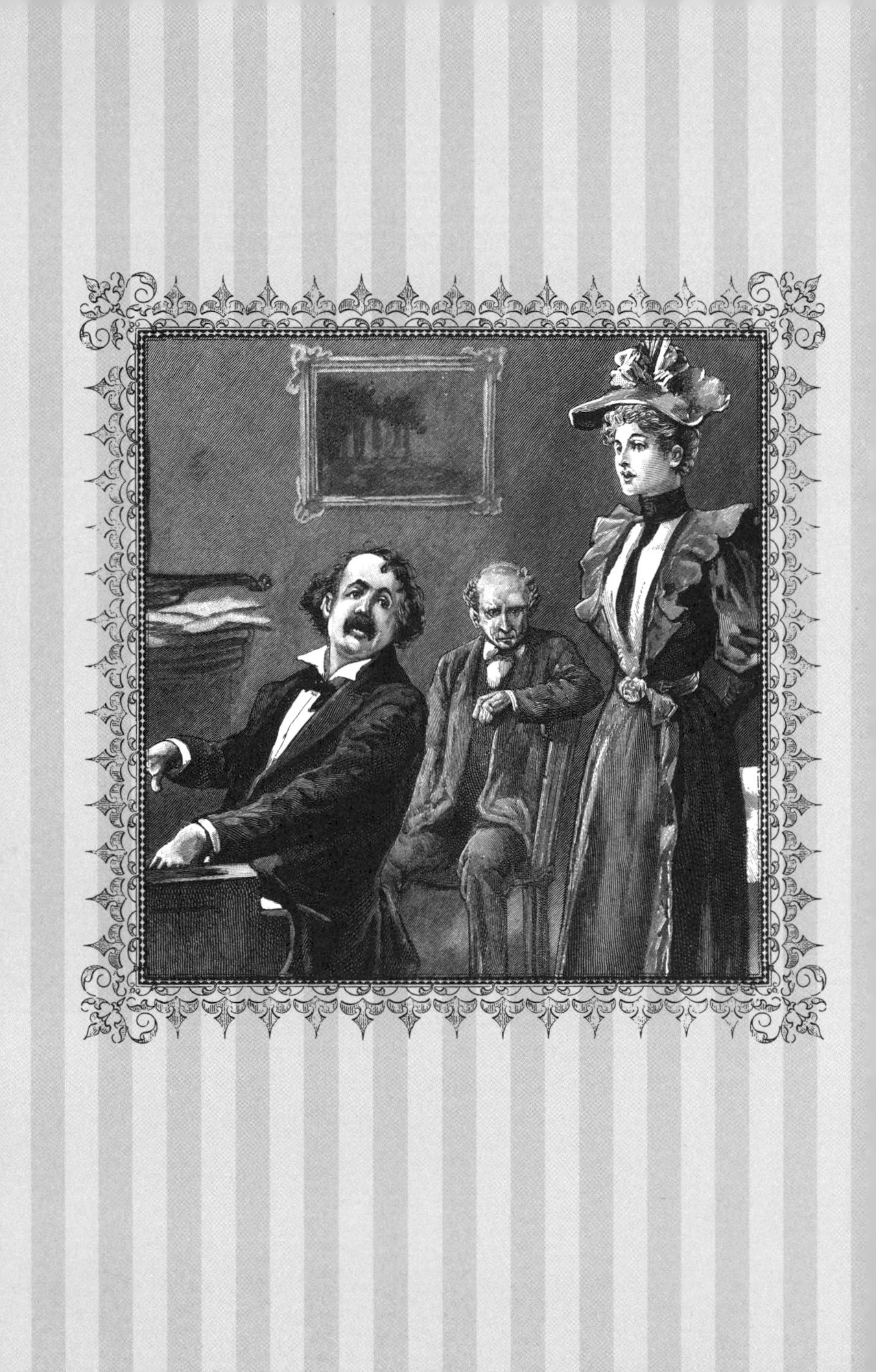

PRACTICE HOURS

Agnes Barden Dustin

Uncle Elgar was coming, and he would take one of the three sisters to Paris. How wonderful it would be! So two of them practiced their music in order to impress him.

The third—well, the third noticed something disturbing in Grandfather.

"It was a long-distance call. From Uncle Elgar!" Lynda informed the family breathlessly from the doorway.

Five pairs of eyes, expressing varying degrees of surprise and curiosity, were lifted from the breakfast table.

"What did he say?" asked Mother.

"He's coming soon!" emphasized Lynda. "In time for a particular event. I don't know what that means," she said, puzzled, "unless it's the old folks' concert tomorrow night. But the great thing is, he's going to take one of us girls to Paris—to *Paris,* mind you!—for three months. He says his voice needs a rest. Going to take the one who 'has made the most progress in the highest of arts,' were his very words. And then he said he would see us soon, and that was all."

"Well, of all things!" breathed Helene, the youngest of the three sisters. "If I'm not thankful I've been taking lessons of Conti and practicing three hours a day! I can finish off that sonata in B-flat if I work very hard. I'll begin as soon as breakfast is finished." Her dark, vivacious face acquired a triumphant expression as she airily fingered an imaginary violin and swept a bow across its strings.

"I shall polish up all my latest songs," put in Lynda quickly. "Of course Uncle Elgar, being a singer himself, has always been greatly interested in my progress in vocal culture."

"Remember, there can't but one of you go," cautioned their mother. "Don't set your hearts on the trip until one is chosen."

"Better look over their clothes, Emily, and have things in readiness," Father advised, as he pushed back his chair and glanced at his watch. "When Elgar takes a notion to go anywhere, he's off without any preliminaries."

Cynthia, the gray-eyed eldest daughter, arose quietly from her place to fetch her father's hat, and search for his spectacle case among the papers on the living-room table. After the hall door had slammed, she did not return to the breakfast-room, from which excited talk flowed like a chattering brook, but made her way slowly upstairs to her own room. When her mother bustled in, a quarter of an hour later, Cynthia was sitting silently by the window, looking out over the garden.

"Cynthia, will you look over the girls' dresses with me? And don't you think we'd better attend that white sale of Pierson's? There is so much to be done that—why, what is the matter, my child? Aren't you feeling well?"

"It doesn't seem to me as if things were very fairly evened up in this family," Cynthia summed up the result of her thoughts, winking away a tear she refused to acknowledge. "I've sewed for the girls since I was out of high school, and done their shares of the housework, and gone without books that I wanted, so that they might have new music and lessons and concert dresses. And now for Uncle Elgar to—just because I'm not musical—oh, it isn't fair! And nobody knows how I've longed to travel and see something!"

"Why, daughter, I never knew you to—"

"Oh, I know, Mother; and I'm ashamed. I'm not really envious of the girls; only, think of going to Paris and the great art museums, and—"

"It was always my dream to travel," her mother admitted.

Cynthia blinked away another tear and looked up into her mother's face. What she saw there of longing, of patience, of weariness, stilled her own disturbed spirit.

"Perhaps the time has come to tell you, daughter, of what you mean to this family," her mother said, sitting down beside her on the window seat, and taking her lax hands in a firm clasp. "You are the mainstay of the home, Cynthia. What could I do without you? You furnish the strength and the clear brain to help me carry out all our household plans and economies, and to keep the younger girls at their lessons until they are fitted to find places for themselves by and by."

"I know—"

"Father works hard at the office and your typewriting his papers at home gives him the little leisure he has in the evenings. Grandfather finds all the brightness and comfort in life, I do believe, in your love and ministrations."

"O Mother, I never meant—"

"You are only a young girl yourself," her mother went on evenly, "not two years older than Lynda, and I fear we rely too much upon your unselfishness and accept too much at your hands; but after all, there is no life like the life of service, and no higher or nobler position a daughter can fill than the place you have made for yourself in this family."

"Now, Mother, as if that were not reward enough for anyone? I'll be good," laughed Cynthia. "All I wanted was a dose of sweet flattery, and I surely received it. Now I'm as serene as the morning and happy as that song sparrow down there on the rosebush."

After her mother had left the room to interview the grocer's boy, Cynthia's hand went out to an old, old Book on the little table beside the sunny window. As she turned its worn pages marked here and there in many readings, a sweetness of expression stole over the young face that matched the freshness and peace of the morning garden below.

Half an hour later, the living-room made tidy and fragrant with flowers, Cynthia went out to sweep the back porch. This was her grandfather's favorite retreat, and here she found him now, sitting in his armchair in the sun, his old dog lying at his feet; but the old man's eyes were closed, and his newspaper had dropped to the floor unheeded.

Wonderingly, Cynthia put her hand on his shoulder. "Is anything the matter, Grandfather? Don't you feel well?"

The old man came back to the present with a start. "Why, no, nothing's the matter, child; of course not. Everything's all right. Are we in your way? We'll move, so you can sweep. Get up, Samp," he said to the grizzled hound. "You're getting as lazy and worthless as your old master."

Cynthia sat down on the arm of the split-bottomed chair, and bent to stroke the old dog's fine head.

Worthless? Of what was her grandfather thinking? Had they neglected him in any way? He was aggrieved over something, that was certain. Cynthia determined to find out what.

"Isn't it great that Uncle Elgar is coming so soon?" she ventured. "You love so to hear him sing, and he's always writing about you and talking with you when he's here, until Mother is actually jealous, I do believe."

"He used to, Cynthy. But I don't take the interest in things I did once. I'm all passed by. Elgar is a good boy, and he and your mother are all I've got left out of nine. They've got their own families and their own affairs now. 'Tisn't likely they can give much place in their busy lives to a doddering old father. I'm eighty, too—pret-ty s-soon now. It's no wonder that folks forget," he sighed.

Today! Cynthia's hand flew to her lips to keep back the exclamation. The stammered word had enlightened her. Grandfather's birthday was today. How could they have forgotten it!

Cynthia was thinking. She seemed to be looking at old Samp, but instead she was seeing a table loaded with good things, and in the center a wonderful birthday cake which Grandmother had made, and friends and neighbors filling the room with talk and laughter. Grandmother had died three years before. The next anniversary Grandfather himself had had pneumonia; the next year was the year of the dreadful "flu," and last March Mother had been with Uncle Elgar's wife when little Carl was born. Cynthia's self-reproach lessened at this array of circumstances.

She patted Grandfather's drooping shoulder, nodded mysteriously, and went briskly away to consult her mother.

"It never rains but it pours!" exclaimed that busy woman, as Cynthia explained. "Of course, if Father feels that way, we must do something; but Sarah Martha's got one of her spells, and Aunt Betsey called up a few minutes ago to say that she wanted to come over to spend the day, and she and Sarah Martha are always at swords' points! With Elgar coming, I didn't dare to mention that to Sarah Martha, or she'd have gone home right away; and the girls so excited, and no dinner, and then a party!" Mrs. Brooke sat down wearily, and contemplated her eldest daughter with a despairing frown.

"Sarah Martha mustn't go back on us!" Cynthia exclaimed in consternation. "There's only one way to break her spells, and that is to get her interested in helping someone else. She thinks everything of Grandfather. Perhaps she can be managed. And Aunt Betsey—I'll take the runabout and drive over for her and tell her to bring her best dress. She loves surprises—and helping get ready will take up her attention. Why, it all fits in beautifully, Mother."

"Maybe," her mother said skeptically.

"I'll see to the party," Cynthia promised. "And to Grandfather and Aunt Betsey and Sarah Martha. Don't give them another thought."

"If you can bring harmony out of this confusion, you'll deserve the Victoria Cross," her mother declared, with a dubious shake of her head. Her step, however, was lighter as she went upstairs to prepare the guest room.

Cynthia took a precautionary peep at the back piazza. Then she entered the spotless kitchen and beckoned mysteriously to Sarah Martha.

Sarah Martha was an individual with as many contrary kinks in her mental make-up as there were angles to her bony frame, and a temper as fiery as her hair. She and Mrs. Brooke had been schoolmates and girlhood chums before Mrs. Brooke had gone away to college. Sarah Martha owned a tiny cottage just beyond the Brookes' back yard, and there she spent her nights and such days as she chose not to act as help in the Brooke kitchen. There was never any word of wages, but weekly Mrs. Brooke called at the immaculate cottage, and on her departure left on the well-scoured table a bill enfolded in a white envelope. Such faithful service through sickness and stress, as Sarah Martha had rendered, could not be paid for in mere coin, and in spite of her kinks and numerous neighborhood quarrels, every member of the Brooke family was her loyal friend and staunch supporter.

The truculence went out of Sarah Martha's quick blue eyes, and the upslant of the coarse red hair seemed to lay itself down as the good woman looked at the disconsolate figure in the worn armchair in the sunshine.

"What's the matter with 'im?" she demanded, shutting the kitchen door with emphasis. "He looks as if he's lost his last friend on earth. 'Tisn't just because I told him to take his old dog out of my kitchen, now?" she recalled with compunction.

"Partly that, no doubt," agreed Cynthia with diplomacy. "And it's his birthday today, and he thinks no one remembers it, and as you say, thinks he hasn't many friends, I guess."

Friends! Sarah Martha's kind heart was enlisted at once. "And who should have more, the good old saint he is! Didn't he give me an organ to play on when I was a girl! I've never forgotten that, and never shall. And many's a time he's used some of his pension money to help me out of a hard place when Mother was alive, God bless 'im! Friends! There ain't a person in this town that's done so much for it as him."

"Let's get them together, then, and give him a surprise party tonight and cheer him up, Sarah Martha. I'll help if you will."

"You leave me to run the thing," Sarah Martha ordered. "Forgot, he thinks he is, the poor old dear! You hustle right along now and invite 'em here for tonight. There ain't a man, woman, or child in this village that don't owe him something, if it's only a good word; and it's paytime. You tell 'em so from me."

"There's Aunt Betsey. Maybe he'd like to have his only sister—"

"She's a nuisance, but if he wants her, fetch her along. And now let me get at that birthday cake."

Peace being restored in the kitchen, Cynthia spent a full hour at the telephone, and then, after the white sale had been attended, drove away for Aunt Betsey and the best dress.

A new atmosphere crept around Grandfather with the coming of that fussy little lady—an atmosphere of mystery and intrigue that aroused Grandfather's curiosity, and awakened a vague expectation that straightened his bowed shoulders and brought a light to his faded eyes, which caused Sarah Martha to sniffle all unseen behind the pantry door.

Grandfather's expectations were strengthened to a certainty of pending pleasures when, just before dinner time, his son Elgar arrived with all the bustle and hearty greetings which usually attended that famous singer's appearance in his home town.

"I suppose the great event which brought you home was the

old folks' concert tomorrow night?" Lynda inquired as, flushed and breathless, she ran downstairs to greet her uncle.

Trills and quavers and scales, issuing industriously through her door nearly all day, had floated down the stairs to meet the ascending trills and quavers and scales from the living-room, where Helene had assiduously practiced her sonata. Both girls were flushed and tired and nervous, but each felt certain of victory.

"Why, no, I can't say that I'd heard of the concert," Uncle Elgar declared. "It was a much more important event which brought me home." He smiled mysteriously at his father as he shook hands again, and told him he was looking as fit as a fiddle.

"What does he mean?" whispered Helene to her mother.

"He expects a big celebration of his father's birthday," answered her mother worriedly. "And I've been so busy I've hardly given it a thought. Cynthia was going to ask in a few friends; but I don't know—"

"What shall we do?" gasped Lynda. "If Uncle is disappointed in us—"

"Have you ordered ice cream?" Uncle Elgar asked in muffled tones. He seemed to think that whispering groups of relatives were a proper part of the proceedings. "Of course not, for all that crowd!" he corrected himself hastily, noting the girls' hesitation. "That's going to be my treat. I'll see Sarah Martha at once." As he departed kitchenward, the two girls fled upstairs.

At dinner time the family had recovered its tranquility. Cynthia had been interviewed, Aunt Betsey had been questioned, and Sarah Martha offered assistance if need should arise. The day was saved. All was well. Helene and Lynda, in crisp organdy, sat one on either side of Uncle Elgar at the table and talked of art and Paris.

Sarah Martha would brook no lingering over the dining-table

that night. Fairly shooed from the room, the family laughingly made pleasant the big front parlors with firelight and lamplight, while Aunt Betsey hurried Grandfather away to be fittingly adorned for the occasion. Then even before the last excited preparations were completed, the earliest guests began to arrive. How they poured in, friends and neighbors, old and new, all eager to grasp Grandfather's hands and wish him joy!

Not a moment dragged of that merry evening. Cynthia's face showed her satisfaction as she ministered to the needs of the guests and heard them vying with one another to recall to Grandfather's mind all of his services to the town, and his many acts of kindness to neighbors during their long years of life together. Uncle Elgar, who had held a private conference with Sarah Martha, watched, with a curiously shrewd smile on his handsome face, the girl talking into the ear trumpet of deaf old Deacon Briggs, and suggesting games for the children present.

Not a trace of the morning's discontent clouded Cynthia's smile of acquiescence when called upon to turn the music for Helene's much practiced sonata and Lynda's songs. For the day had brought wisdom, and Cynthia had found the antidote for disappointment and mediocrity of talent in a calm content in filling her own place. Her mother's words and the experiences of that memorable birthday had crystallized her growing belief that the secret of real happiness and success is in the giving out of love in service to have it return to fill the heart of the giver with joy and hope, and a yet greater love. So it was no wonder that some of her inward happiness made her face sweet and bright that evening.

When Uncle Elgar had sung to them in his wonderful tenor voice, and had granted seemingly endless petitions for certain favorites, plaintive melodies of the South, old Scottish songs, and ballads which have endured, the party broke up reluctantly, and the guests trooped out into the starry night. The home folks put out the brilliant lights and gathered about the glowing embers in the fireplace to reminisce about the evening. Then it was that something happened, something totally unexpected.

"I hope the one who is responsible for this delightful birthday party will consent to cheer up her old uncle on his travels," the famous tenor said, laying a hand on Cynthia's shoulder. "There is no art so high as the art of living, and this little girl has learned to take her instrument of life to the Great Master for tuning, and the resultant harmony is very sweet."

Agnes Barden Dustin

Agnes Barden Dustin wrote for inspirational magazines during the first half of the twentieth century.

HIS LEGACY

Bill Gaither
with Jerry B. Jenkins

The old man wouldn't sell. But he did have a question of his own to ask. A question that made all the difference.

Benjy and I were working in the yard together one afternoon. It was during a summer between college terms, a time of uncertainty for my son. Benjy wanted to follow in my footsteps as a musician, but he was impatient for success. I ached for him and wished I could say something.

Taking a break, Benjy looked around our fifteen acres with its stream, its trees, its rolling grass. "This place is beautiful," he said wistfully. "How did you get it?"

"I wondered when you'd ask," I replied. We tend to take things for granted until we're about to leave or lose them. I told Benjy the story.

Our first child, Suzanne, had just been born. Gloria and I were teaching in Alexandria, Indiana, where I had grown up. We wanted land so we could build a house.

I noticed a parcel south of town where cattle grazed. It belonged to a ninety-two-year-old retired banker named Mr. Yule. He owned a lot of land in the area, but was selling none of it. He gave the same speech to everyone who inquired: "I promised the farmers they could use it for their cattle."

Nevertheless, Gloria and I visited him at the bank, where he still spent his days. Little Suzanne was in tow, bonnet in place. We made our way past a forbidding mahogany door and into a dim office. Mr. Yule sat behind a desk, reading *The Wall Street Journal.* He barely moved, looking at us over the top of his bifocals.

"Not selling," he said pleasantly, when I told him we were interested in the piece of land. "Promised it to a farmer for grazing."

"I know," I replied nervously. "But we teach school here, and we thought that maybe you would sell it to someone planning to settle."

He pursed his lips and stared. "What'd you say your name was?"

"Gaither. Bill Gaither."

"H'mmm. Any relation to Grover Gaither?"

"Yes, sir. He was my granddad."

Mr. Yule put down his paper and removed his glasses. Then he pointed to a couple of chairs, and we sat down.

"Grover Gaither was the best worker I ever had on my farm," he said. "Showed up early, stayed late, did whatever needed doing and never had to be told."

The old man leaned forward. "I found him in the barn one night an hour after quitting time. Told me the tractor needed fixing and he wouldn't feel right about leaving it undone." Mr. Yule squinted, his eyes distant with the memory. "What'd you say you wanted, Gaither?"

I told him again.

"Let me do some thinking on it, then come back and see me."

I was in his office again within a week. "How does $3,800 sound?" he asked.

At $3,800 per acre, I would have to come up with nearly $60,000! Was this just a way of putting me off?

"Thirty-eight hundred?" I repeated, with a catch in my throat.

"Yup. Fifteen acres for $3,800." *The land had to be worth at least three times that!* I gratefully accepted.

Nearly three decades later, my son and I strolled the lush property that had once been pasture. "Benjy," I said, "you've had this wonderful place to grow up on all because of the good name of a man you never met."

At Granddad's funeral, many people had come up to me to say, "Your grandfather was a good man." He was praised for his compassion, his ability to forgive, his tenderness, his generosity—and, most of all, his integrity. He had been a simple farmer, but his character made him a leader.

A good man. A wonderful phrase—one that has almost been lost in our culture. It reminds me of a verse from Proverbs that I was raised on: "A good name is rather to be chosen than great riches, and loving favor rather than silver and gold."

A good name is the legacy Granddad Gaither left me. It is what I hope to leave Benjy, along with a story he can tell his son as they walk this gentle land.

Bill Gaither and Jerry B. Jenkins

Bill Gaither and his wife, Gloria, are two of the best-known inspirational musicians of our time. They still live in his native Indiana. Jerry B. Jenkins is coauthor of the best-selling Left Behind series.

THE COUSINS' CONSPIRACY

Helen Ward Banks

Phyllis and Ted were troubled. Grandmother had everything in the world that money could buy, and she had family and a host of servants to implement her every wish. But why wasn't she happy? Why didn't she sing anymore?

They set out to find the reason.

Phyllis rose from the breakfast table as Aunt Ellen pushed back her chair. "Shall I ring for Collins, Aunt Ellen?" she asked.

"Please," Mrs. Winter answered absently, "and see if you can find my gloves, Phylly. I haven't had time to give any orders. Will you see Cook? Anything I can do for you in town, Mother?"

"I don't need anything, thank you," Grandmother answered, with her patient smile.

Aunt Ellen took her gloves from Phyllis. "Thank you. Shall you be here for lunch, Phylly?"

"I wasn't intending to," Phyllis answered. "Ted's coming today, you know. I was going to drive over for him this morning, stay to lunch with Aunt Molly, and bring Ted back this afternoon. But I can let Collins go if Grandmother minds."

"Not at all, my dear," Grandmother said. "I don't in the least mind being alone."

"Well, you arrange it, Phylly," Aunt Ellen said vaguely, "and have Sarah make a room ready for Ted. Order any meals you like. I'll be back for dinner. Good-by, Mother."

She dropped a casual kiss on her mother's cheek as she passed, patted Phyllis's shoulder, and was off for a busy and useful day in town. Aunt Ellen might neglect to order dinner and forget to go to bed, but no one could deny that with her orphan asylums and old-ladies' homes, she did a great deal to help humanity.

Phyllis scrambled around for an hour or two, ordering meals and filling the rooms with spring flowers—tulips and daffodils and jonquils. Grandmother sat in the morning-room, patiently reading the paper, while she waited for Sarah to put her room in order. She was aching to do it herself, but that was not allowable in a house filled with servants.

"Aren't they pretty, Grandmother?" Phyllis asked as she set down her last jug. "But I do want some narcissi terribly, and there isn't one in bloom. The place was white with them when they grew in the lower garden; but I wanted them where I could see them, and Aunt Ellen let Boylston transplant them up here under the windows two years ago, and not a blossom have they showed since. Why do you suppose they act like that?"

"Probably they didn't like transplanting," suggested Grandmother. "Some things don't."

"But these bulbs had been transplanted once already to the lower garden."

"Then probably it's a matter of soil. I never could raise Canterbury bells in my garden, while my neighbor had a thicket of them."

"What a lovely garden you had, though!" Phyllis remarked. "I should think you'd miss it dreadfully, Grandmother."

"I'd be very ungrateful to miss anything, shouldn't I, when Ellen gives me so much here?"

"She is good to us both, isn't she?" Phyllis declared. "I love it here; don't you?"

"It is very beautiful," said Grandmother.

"And yet," declared Phyllis shrewdly, "I have a feeling that you aren't really happy. Didn't you want to come here?"

"Of course I wanted to," Grandmother said hastily. "There is no one I'm happier with than you and Ellen. And there was nothing else to do but come here, after Nelly married. It would have been foolish for me to try to live on in Weston when Ellen had this big place with only you and her in it. It would have made all my children uneasy to think of me being alone, and I shouldn't have liked it myself."

"I suppose that's true," pondered Phyllis, "but somehow you

don't seem to have taken root, exactly. Will you drive over with me for Ted?"

"No thank you, dear. It's a pretty long ride and you drive pretty fast. I'm more used to the pace of Brown Bess, you know."

Phyllis laughed. "I used to play Indian on Brown Bess's back. But nobody could drive a horse nowadays in such a welter of automobiles. Why don't you learn to drive a car, Grandmother?"

"They go so fast," hesitated Grandmother. "I could if it wasn't for that."

Phyllis kissed her. "Precious thing! I hate to leave you all alone. I'm going to ask Miss Lamson to lunch with you."

"Don't," protested Grandmother. "I shouldn't know what to say to her."

"Well then, there's a Ladies' Aid meeting this afternoon at Mrs. Brown's. I heard it given out Sunday. Let Collins take you to that."

Grandmother shook her head. "No, I haven't joined the Ladies' Aid. I wouldn't want to unless I could entertain them, and I couldn't here."

"Aunt Ellen would love to have you do so."

"Yes. But I never could be sure that, the day I invited the Society, Ellen wouldn't want the parlor for a boys' club or something. I wouldn't have an easy moment."

Phyllis laughed again. "I've got to be off now or I'll get no lunch anywhere. If you want anything, there's Collins and Saunders and Sarah and Lisa."

"They aren't mine," breathed Grandmother, "but I won't need anything. Run along now, darling, or you will be late. I'm glad Ted is coming; he's a fine boy."

"The nicest cousin I have," agreed Phyllis. "We'll be home early."

Phyllis was not smiling as she started her car. She carried instead a little perplexed wrinkle between her pretty brows. Grandmother never fretted, and Phyllis was waking up to the fact that she was not happy. What was it that was wrong?

She forgot her problem while she ate a jolly luncheon with Aunt Molly and Ted; but when she and Ted started toward home it came back, and she shared it with her cousin. Ted rubbed the back of his head in perplexity.

"You've got me," he declared. "I don't know why she should be unhappy. It looks as if she had everything she could want, and she's a pretty good old sport."

"I adore her!" Phyllis said. "And she told me that she liked being with us. She does. But she isn't happy the way she used to be. Don't you remember how she always used to be puttering about and singing?"

Ted nodded. " 'How firm a foundation, ye saints of the Lord,' " he sang. "When you heard that, you knew that everything was top-notch."

"And she never sings now," mourned Phyllis. "We must find out what's the matter, Ted."

"We'll try to dope it out," Ted responded.

They found Grandmother alone on the veranda, with her usual affectionate smile for her grandchildren. Ted dropped his hat on a chair and stooped to kiss her.

"Have a good day, Grandmother?" Phyllis asked.

"Yes, dear. Letitia Brown and her sister drove over from Weston to see me."

"How nice!" Phyllis exclaimed.

Grandmother laughed a little ruefully. "Yes. I was glad to hear all the town gossip; but I'm afraid they won't come again. My grand surroundings frightened them some, especially when Saunders brought in that big tea tray."

"I guess they'll get over it and come again," Phyllis comforted her. "See, Ted, that's the bed of narcissi that won't bloom. Grandmother thinks that they don't like the soil."

"That's easily fixed," Ted answered. "Tomorrow morning we'll dig them out and fill in the bed with three or four wheelbarrow-loads of the soil that they used to blossom in."

"Oh, Ted! Would you? This really is the place for them."

"Sure thing!" Ted said. "Want a set of tennis before dinner?"

"Sure thing!" laughed Phyllis, and the two young people went off together.

But when they reached the tennis court Ted dropped himself to a grassy bank. "Listen here, Phyl," he said. "I've dug out the answer to your question about Granny. It's in your narcissus bed."

"What do you mean?" puzzled Phyllis.

"You want those narcissi to blossom near the house; it's the right place for them to blossom. You transplant them there and they take hold, but they won't blossom; it isn't the right kind of soil to make flowers. We won't take them back to the lower garden; we'll bring lower garden soil up to them."

"Well, what then?" questioned Phyllis.

"We've transplanted Granny from her own little home with one servant into Aunt Ellen's big house where you step on a maid or a man every time you lift a foot. It's utterly foreign soil to Granny. She's striking root because she's a sport, but she hasn't anything left to blossom with. She isn't living her own life at all; she's living yours and Aunt Ellen's."

"Of course!" acceded Phyllis. "That's insightful of you, Ted!

But where are we going to get three or four wheelbarrows full of old soil to dump into her new flower bed?"

Ted turned over on his elbow and began to pluck spears of grass. "We can certainly dope it out," he replied thoughtfully. "We have our starting point. We can see that Granny isn't planted in her own garden, but in a corner of yours and Aunt Ellen's."

Phyllis nodded. "We didn't mean to be selfish, but that's true."

"I don't believe it's a question of selfishness," Ted returned slowly. "Granny doesn't want more of your life and Aunt Ellen's; she wants her own, where she can do as she darned pleases. Isn't there some place in that big, rambling house that she could have all to herself, bedroom and bath, sitting-room and kitchenette, so that she could make her friends a cup of tea when they come to see her without frightening them off the face of the earth by waving Saunders at them?"

Phyllis clasped her hands: "Edward Carpenter, you blessed angel! Of course there is. There is that ell in the east wing that Aunt Ellen built on for one of her protégées once. There are—let's see—one, two, three—there are five rooms in it: two bedrooms and a bath, a good big sitting-room, and a little brick walk outside. Ted, it's made for her!"

"Would she need a servant?" Teddy asked.

"No, it would bother her to have someone around all the time. She likes housework. She used to make her own bed here till Aunt Ellen stopped her. Oh, and Ted, she could get her own breakfast whenever she wanted; she always waits hours for us, and she refuses to have it sent to her room. And she hates late dinners. She could come to lunch, you see—that's always a hearty meal—and she could get her own supper the way she likes it."

"If there are two bedrooms, she could have Letitia for a visit," Ted suggested with a grin.

"And the Ladies' Aid! I know she misses it. Oh, Ted, why have we been so stupid! One of the maids will keep the place clean for her, and if she wants to have company, she can have all her meals cooked on her own stove. Lisa is devoted to Grandmother; she'd always be ready to help her out."

"It's going to work," affirmed Ted. "Aunt Ellen won't mind."

"She'll think it's a wonderful idea, for don't you see, Grandmother will be connected with the house and yet be perfectly independent. She can have her own garden too. She loves muddling in a garden. Now if she only had her old horse again, she'd be just like old times."

"Horses aren't safe to drive nowadays," Ted mused, "but she ought to have some way to get around." He plucked a few more grass-blades and then sat erect. "Why, that's easy! Mother is learning to drive a gas car; we'll make her give her electric[5] to Granny."

"She could drive that," breathed Phyllis. "And she'd love it. Oh, Ted, wouldn't your mother ask her over for a week and teach her to drive the electric while we get the place ready?"

"Sure thing! We'll call her up tonight after we've told Aunt Ellen. Now how about furniture?"

"There'll be plenty of furniture," promised Phyllis.

"What became of Granny's furniture?" Ted asked.

"She gave it away when she came here. It was ugly stuff—black walnut in hideous shapes."

"We think so. But I believe Granny likes it. It's the soil she's used to, anyhow. Do you suppose we could get it back, Phyl?"

"Teddy!" exclaimed Phyllis. "You're a perfect genius. We'll

[5] *Electric cars could not go as fast as gas-powered cars and were comparatively easy to drive.*

take the little truck and go to Weston tomorrow and march up and down the village street until we get back the whole lot of it."

"You've said it!" Ted exclaimed, jumping to his feet and extending a helping hand to Phyllis. "Now it's tennis. Tonight you can tackle Aunt Ellen while I spring the plan on Mother."

Aunt Ellen gave Phyllis *carte blanche* with the east wing, and Aunt Molly jumped into the plan with all her generous heart. She called Grandmother up that very evening to ask for an immediate visit while Ted was away, and Grandmother accepted it as patiently as she accepted everything that was done for her.

Collins carried her off the next morning, and no sooner was she gone than carpenters and plumbers appeared in the east wing. Boylston was dragged from the job he was at to dig flower borders by the new front door and to set out lilacs and syringas and snowballs in the new little dooryard. Then, the work well started, Ted and Phyllis snatched an early lunch, mounted the farm truck, and rumbled over to Weston to look up Letitia Brown.

They found Letitia an eager ally. She herself had the dining-table, which she helped Ted load into the truck. She went with them to the minister, who gladly gave up the parlor sofa, and to the doctor, who returned Grandmother's best bedroom set. At the end of the street they had salvaged all that the new apartment could hold, even down to the parlor carpet. Everything was restored, with blessings on the hand that had given it, and Ted and Phyllis drove triumphantly home.

Wonders had been accomplished in their absence. Boylston had every shrub in place and the borders filled with new plants. He had cut the grass and swept the brick walk, and now was carting soil from the lower garden to the narcissus bed. The plumbers had set a new sink in the kitchen, fitted the pipe for the gas stove, and removed the bathroom fixtures to make room for new. The carpenter had installed the kitchen cabinet, put in shelves, and shut off the apartment from the main house by a door. And tomorrow was a new day!

Ted and Phyllis were unflagging taskmasters. In five days they had the repairs made, the rooms papered and painted, and finally scrubbed and scoured. When they had turned out the last worker the parlor carpet was laid, the rosewood set moved in on it, and the old pictures hung. The dining-room, too, and Grandmother's bedroom and the guest-room all looked as if, like Birnam Wood at Dunsinane, they had moved themselves bodily from Grandmother's old life. Only the kitchen was new, shining in blue and white, with a new sink and a new gas range and a new white porcelain table, and many, many new gleaming utensils.

When it was done to the last pin in the pincushion and the pad over the telephone, Aunt Ellen went over it, with tears in her kindly, far-gazing eyes.

"It's perfect, Phylly!" she murmured. "Why didn't we think of it months ago?"

That night they telephoned Aunt Molly that they would send for Grandmother the next morning.

"There's no need to send," Aunt Molly said. "Mother will drive me over in the electric. She drives it beautifully. Have Collins find a place for it and for the charging apparatus. It's my contribution to the new garden you are planting."

"We aren't planting the garden—just dumping in the right soil," laughed Phyllis. "Grandmother is going to plant the garden."

They were all waiting for Grandmother the next morning when she drove up proudly with Aunt Molly. Aunt Ellen and Phyllis and Ted were on the veranda, Saunders and Lisa and Sarah all hovering in the hall, Collins waiting to take the electric, and Boylston finding it necessary to trim the roses by the drive-way. Even Cook chose that moment to come for orders.

Grandmother, bright-eyed, descended from her chariot. "Do you see what a wonderful present Molly has given me?" she asked Phyllis.

"It's a day of presents!" Phyllis exclaimed, hugging her. "Come and see what Aunt Ellen has for you."

Phyllis and Ted, each with a hand, pulled Grandmother forward, Aunt Ellen and Aunt Molly followed, and all the servants brazenly trailed behind. Everybody was smiling as Ted opened the door and Grandmother faced her new home.

For a minute Grandmother turned white; then she was crying and laughing and exploring, while Aunt Ellen dropped a few tears and everyone else laughed and almost pulled Grandmother to pieces trying to show her everything at once. They ended in the new, bright little kitchen, where Grandmother opened drawers and peeped into cupboards and lit her gas stove, like a little girl with her first baby-house.

"You blessed, blessed children!" she kept exclaiming. "How could you know how an old woman's heart yearns for just her own? Oh, you blessed children!"

"I remember some ginger cookies about a hundred years ago," Ted observed reminiscently. "I've dreamed about them ever since."

Grandmother turned to the trim apron that hung beside the kitchen cabinet. "I'll make that dream come true in a jiffy," she said.

Still wiping her eyes, Aunt Ellen took Aunt Molly back to the veranda, the servants drifted away, and Ted and Phyllis sat down on the steps of the little kitchen porch, listening to Grandmother moving about within. Presently through the open window came Grandmother's voice singing in her low, happy tone:

"How firm a foundation, ye saints of the Lord."

Phyllis leaned over and grasped Ted's hand. "Do you hear?" she whispered. "The soil is right, and the garden is planted. It's beginning to blossom!"

Helen Ward Banks

Helen Ward Banks, born in Brooklyn, New York, wrote for the family and popular markets during the first half of the twentieth century. Among her books are *The Boynton Pluck* (1904), *The House of the Lions* (1924), and *The Story of Mexico* (1926).

THE DELAYED LETTER

Elizabeth Ann Tollmann

Richard couldn't understand why his grandfather should have made such a ridiculous request of him. Why, he'd be the laughingstock of the entire campus!

For a moment Richard Lipton looked dazedly at the yellow slip of paper which had just been handed to him by the messenger boy. Again he read the words: "Richard Lipton, Harvard College. Come immediately. Grandfather not expected to live. S. R. Saunders, M.D."

The words cut deep into the boy's heart. Only a month more, and then the Christmas holidays would be here, and Richard had planned a merry vacation to be spent with two of his college friends at his grandfather's luxurious home. His grandfather had written him to bring any of his friends he might choose, and had given him a hint of the many pleasant times he had planned for them. But it was not the thwarting of these happy expectations which made the boy's face grow pale; ah, no, but rather because Jarius Martin Lipton had taken the place of both father and mother to the little curly-haired grandson who had been bereft of both parents when the ocean steamer on which they were traveling had been wrecked off the coast of Australia. Though Jarius Lipton might be stern and unbending to others, his grandson held the key to his heart, and upon him he had lavished all the wealth of a deep love. Yet, remembering ruefully some of his experiences, Richard had to confess that his grandfather had not spoiled him.

Mechanically he made arrangements for his trip. The hours seemed an eternity as the train sped onward, but finally the long journey was over. The great house on the hill seemed deathly quiet and silent when the young man arrived. The old Scotch housekeeper met him at the door, saying as she took his hand, "Ah, laddie, it's a sad, sad day."

"How is Grandfather?" anxiously inquired Richard.

"I don't think you would have seen him had you been a day later," was her answer. "I'll go now and find out if you can see him."

In a moment she returned. "Doctor says for you to come in, but go still, lad," she said.

In the dim light Richard saw the doctor sitting by the bed, with a finger on Mr. Lipton's pulse; the nurse, in white gown and cap, stood near, with a tiny glass of medicine in her hand. The doctor silently motioned for Richard to come near, and the boy knelt by his grandfather's bed and bowed his head in his hands. Mr. Lipton opened his eyes and saw his boy, and all the yearning affection of a father for his son was in his eyes as he whispered, "I'm so glad you're here, Dickie." For a few moments he rested content, his free hand clasping Richard's, then again he spoke, slowly and painfully. "Dickie—I'm going to leave—you—I think, but—I've left word—for you with—the lawyer. Promise—you'll do what—I ask you to—when he tells you." Kneeling there by the side of the one who had done everything for him, it was easy enough for Richard to make the promise. At the setting of the sun, Jarius Lipton's long, eventful life came to a close.

The day Richard was to return to college, Mr. Weston, the lawyer, telephoned to him, asking him to come to the office. Mr. Weston greeted the boy kindly and with tender sympathy, for Mr. Lipton and the lawyer had been lifelong friends.

"It's your grandfather's will, Richard, that you should know about," he explained, and then he began reading the document. Mr. Lipton had been a generous and philanthropic man who had taken delight in doing good with the great wealth entrusted to him, and there were many bequests and legacies to friends and institutions. Although Richard followed the lawyer as he read through the legal phraseology, it was not until he heard the following words that his mind was brought to a focus upon what was being read:

"To my beloved grandson, Richard Ellsworth Lipton, I give

and bequeath the residue of my estate, both real and personal, to him, his heirs, and his assigns forever, with this condition: That he shall not come into control of the said estate for a period of ten years following my death, and no benefits of said estate shall accrue to him beyond an amount of money necessary for him to complete his education, said expenditure of money to be under control of John L. Weston.

"I give and bequeath to my grandson, Richard Ellsworth Lipton, my black broadcloth overcoat, with the request that he wear it during the school year at Harvard University, and that when wearing said overcoat he shall not wear gloves, giving no explanation therefor."

As the lawyer concluded these words, Richard's countenance expressed astonishment and bewilderment. His grandfather's black broadcloth overcoat! Why, since he could remember he had never seen his grandfather wear any other coat, of a style which had not been worn for twenty-five years. Jarius Lipton had clung affectionately to his coat in spite of all his grandson had urged to the contrary. "An overcoat isn't like other clothes, Dick," he had said. "It's good just as long as it is good. There isn't a thing the matter with that coat. Maybe it isn't right up to the minute in style, but what of that? It is warm and comfortable, and that is all that is necessary." And Richard had consoled himself with the thought that his grandfather could do things that would be considered freakish in other people, and yet not be thought any the less of by his friends. But to ask *him* to wear that coat! It was preposterous!

"Mr. Weston, I don't understand," he finally said. "Was—do you think—are you quite sure Grandfather was in his right mind when he wrote that last statement?"

The lawyer smiled. "Yes, Dick, he was," was his answer. Then he gave the boy a keen glance. "Did he ask you to promise anything before he died?"

Richard started as he remembered the last few words of his grandfather. "Yes, and I promised," he said slowly.

"This is what he had reference to," the lawyer explained. "You know, my boy, your grandfather was a little eccentric and had some queer ideas, but if you promised, I believe you are man enough to keep your promise." Mr. Weston gripped hard the young man's hand as he spoke the words.

Richard Lipton returned to Harvard that evening, reluctantly taking the black overcoat with him. He tried in vain to overcome the resentment that crept into his heart. Why had his grandfather taken advantage of him in this way? What was his object in thus trying to humiliate him? For this request of Mr. Lipton's had touched Richard upon his weakest spot. He was fastidious about his personal appearance to the extreme. More than once he remembered his grandfather's saying to him, "Ah, Dick, you are too much of a dude, I'm afraid; don't let it run away with you, my boy." And now that he, Richard Lipton, the best-dressed man in college, should appear in public wearing that old overcoat twenty-five years behind the styles was something beyond comprehension, and yet—there was his promise. If he could only explain to the fellows why he was doing it, it would be all right, but this way—and Richard gritted his teeth.

The weeks passed, and still the black overcoat lay in the bottom of Richard's trunk. Soon the spring days came, and then it was too late to fulfill his promise, and back home with Richard went the black overcoat. Mr. Weston greeted Richard heartily, but made no reference to the request of the will, and Richard vouchsafed no explanation. In the fall when he returned to Harvard, the black overcoat went too. It was not long before his conscience began to torment him. Wherever he was, whatever he did, a vision of that black overcoat rose up before him, and he knew he must make a decision as to what he was going to do.

The sharp days of fall demanded heavy wraps, and one November afternoon Richard fought a battle with himself, finally saying with a laugh, "Oh, pshaw, what do I care what people think? Here goes." And an hour later, wearing the despised coat, and minus gloves, in accordance with the instructions of the will, Richard started downtown. He was nearly past a group of boys before they recognized him, and then one of them exclaimed, "Lipton, what's the idea? Starting something new in styles?" Richard joined in the laugh at his expense, but no questioning from the boys could bring forth any explanation. It was an uncomfortable afternoon for the boy. It seemed to him all his friends were downtown that day, but worst of all was when he met Margaret Standish, the most popular girl in town, with a number of friends. Like the boys, at first they did not recognize Richard, and then Margaret gayly greeted him, but Richard felt, rather than saw, the odd little smile upon the girls' faces. He was miserably conscious of the long dangling garment. But it was not so bad as Richard pictured to himself, for both boys and girls spent a merry time laughing over "Dick's new stunt," as they expressed it.

As he was returning home, Richard's bare fingers began to tingle with the cold, and he thrust his hands into the pockets of the overcoat. His hand came in contact with some paper, which he drew out and found to be an envelope addressed to himself in his grandfather's handwriting. Opening it, he read on the enclosed paper the following words:

DEAR DICK: Somehow I imagine it will be quite a while before you get this letter, for I believe I know my boy pretty well. You have the making of a splendid man in you, Dick, but you care a whole lot too much what folks think of you. Of course a man may be a fashion plate, I suppose, and still be a man, but don't carry it to such an extreme that you are afraid to turn around unless you know you will pass muster at a "spring showing." Perhaps it wouldn't be such a terrible thing if you stopped at clothes, but this principle of being afraid of what folks will think of you unless you are dressed just right is liable to affect you in the more serious things of life. So I have planned this little test for you. You may be a little while getting around to doing what I have asked, but you'll finally do it; I know just how hard it is going to be for you, because you are going to do it without knowing how it is going to end, but you promised, and I've never known you to break a promise. You need not wear the coat again after reading this, but communicate with Mr. Weston immediately. Good luck and success to you, my boy, and may you ever pass as successfully your future tests in life. GRANDFATHER.

Richard was not ashamed of the moisture in his eyes as he finished reading these words. "My, what a cad I've been," he murmured, "but I'm glad I didn't fizzle out altogether."

Mr. Weston smiled when he read the words of the telegram which he received the next day from Dick, and his smile deepened as he dictated the following words in reply: "Congratulations, Dick. You've stood the test. You come into possession of your grandfather's entire estate the day of your graduation from Harvard."

Elizabeth Ann Tollmann

Elizabeth Ann Tollmann wrote for family magazines during the first half of the twentieth century.

READY FOR HEAVEN

Ewart A. Autry

The Grim Reaper was coming for Grandpa. His heart, that heretofore faithful source of life, was now signaling that his life was over—or would be before nightfall. Looking around the house, he decided there were a few things that needed fixing before folks came over for the funeral. There was even a feud that ought to be settled that very hour.

Or so he thought. . . .

It was ten o'clock on a hot June morning when Grandpa Hawkins decided he was about to die. He didn't tell anyone just then, but Grandma knew something was wrong when she saw him grab the lawnmower and start cutting grass. Just a few minutes before she had seen him playing with five of the grandchildren in the shade of the big apple tree. The yard had needed mowing for ten days. She had mentioned it to him several times without visible results. It wasn't like him to suddenly leave the cool shade and go to work just as the sun was getting hot.

She put on her glasses and watched him through a window. Even the grandchildren had left the apple tree and were staring at him in amazement. But he wasn't paying any attention to them. He wasn't noticing anything except the grass. The dog flopped down in front of him and almost got his tail mowed before he could get out of the way. Grandma smiled and went back to her work. *That won't last long,* she said to herself. *He'll be back under the apple tree in no time at all.*

But when she looked out an hour later, the yard was almost finished, and he was still doggedly pushing the mower as if nothing else in the world mattered. A puzzled frown creased her forehead. It always worried her when Grandpa failed to run true to form. It usually meant that some unheard-of scheme was forming in his mind. Like the time he went deer hunting on stilts and fell into a hole. Or the time he dressed like a woman and killed a buck and got his picture in the county paper. Or the time he took the doo-jingle off her new hat and used it for a lure to catch the biggest bass ever caught in the county. Or the time he had become the first skin diver in the county and scared the daylights out of the fishermen up the river. News had circulated that there was a strange creature in the river, and folks had come from miles around to see the monster of Corkscrew Bend. No sir, Grandma had never found life dull with the little sawed-off man with the bristling mustache who was now so industriously mowing the yard.

It is little wonder that she worried as she saw him finishing up the last corner of the yard. There might be something bubbling in his head which would have the whole county laughing. Sometimes his weird ideas had proved downright embarrassing. In a moment, however, she smiled again. *He's probably planning another fishing trip,* she said to herself, *and wants to leave with a clear conscience.*

When the yard was finished, Grandpa came into the house. "Take a peep at the yard, Ma," he said, "and see if it satisfies you."

"I was watching you," she said. "Seems to me that you did a good job."

"Mighty few men, and no boys at all, could beat it," he said briefly.

"Why did you take such a sudden notion to cut it?" she asked curiously. "I've been reminding you that it needed cutting for several days."

"I don't do things when folks keep reminding me to do them," he said testily. "That's plain nagging. I cut it because I got to thinking that I'd hate for a crowd to come in and see the yard looking like a rabbits' den."

"Well, it looks nice, but I don't suppose there'll be a crowd coming in," she said.

"There may be a crowd coming in before you know it," he said significantly.

"You've never before seemed to care what the neighbors thought about the yard," Grandma remarked. "You've always said if they didn't like it they didn't have to look at it."

"There comes a time when a man starts caring for things," he said. "Where's the hammer?"

"In the hall closet where it always stays," she said. "What do you want with it?"

"You always have more questions than I have answers," he snorted. "But if you must know, I'm aiming to fix that back screen door."

She stopped dusting and looked at him closely. "Are you feeling well, Lem?" she asked.

"Maybe I am, and maybe I'm not," he said. "If I am, it's my business. If I'm not, it's the same."

Grandma smiled and went back to her dusting. For forty years she had been accustomed to his crusty, belligerent ways, and knew that beneath that rough exterior there was a faithfulness and tenderness of heart which had made life with him very wonderful. Folks had always said that she spoke softly like the dripping rain, while he roared like thunder, and that thunder and rain went well together.

He pecked away at the screen in silence. There was no muttering and no sudden explosion even when he mashed a finger. When it was finished he called Grandma to see it. "Now I guess folks won't be saying I just let things go around here," he said.

"It's a good job," Grandma told him, "but hardly anyone sees the back door except me."

"There'll probably be a lot of other folks seeing it," he said. "They'd better come!" he added vehemently.

"Lem, have you invited some folks to our house?" she asked. "If you have, I'd better do a little extra cleaning up."

"I haven't invited anybody," he said emphatically, "but there are times when folks come without being invited. I think I'll shave."

Grandma dropped into a chair. "Well, this beats all," she said. "You just shaved last night, and here you are ready to shave again. I don't know what's on your mind, but there's bound to be something—something very unusual."

"Is there any law against a man shaving any time he gets ready?" he demanded.

"Of course not," she said. "It's just that I don't understand it." She shook her head slowly and went into the kitchen. He followed her, opened the refrigerator and took a package from the freezing compartment. "Let's have this steak for dinner," he said.

"But that's those nice T-bone steaks," she said. "I thought we were saving them for some special occasion."

"This *is* a special occasion," he said. "Let's have the T-bones." He scratched his chin for a moment. "We could invite Milt Huggins over to eat them with us," he added.

Grandma dropped a plate and stared at him in amazement. "Now I *know* there's something wrong, Lem Hawkins," she said. "You and Milt Huggins have been feuding for years, and now you are ready to invite him over for a steak dinner!"

"Oh, I guess Milt's all right," he said. "He can't help being hollow-headed, simple-minded, and dumb. I ought not to hold it against him."

"You two are just alike," Grandma said. "It's about time you quit that silly feuding. It makes you the laughingstock of the community."

"I wonder if he'll send flowers?" Grandpa said thoughtfully.

"What on earth are you talking about, Lem?" Grandma asked, now completely baffled, and beginning to wonder if perhaps Grandpa was a little touched in the head.

"I was just wondering if Milt would send flowers to my funeral," he said simply.

"Did you get too hot out there helping the kids catch bugs and things for their circus?" she demanded.

"If I got too hot at all, it was mowing the yard," he said shortly. "Anyhow, my heart was acting up before I cut the grass."

"Your heart?" cried Grandma in alarm.

"Yes, my heart," he said. "It's been thumping and jumping and cutting all sorts of shines. I'm sure I'll go to glory this very day. That's why I thought I'd better cut the yard and fix the screen. If I go suddenly, there'll be a crowd in to sit with you."

Grandma was already pulling off her apron. "You're going to see a doctor, Lem!" she said firmly. "And you're going at once!"

"Now, hold your horses, woman. I aim to eat some of that T-bone steak before I go anywhere. Even when a man's going to the electric chair he gets to choose his last meal. Well, I choose T-bone steaks, and T-bone steaks I aim to eat. No use to leave them around for somebody else to gobble up when I'm lying in the dirt. Think I'll read a chapter in the Bible while you're finishing dinner."

He started for the next room, but stopped in the door and turned. "That's what I'm talking about," he said solemnly, pointing toward the region of his heart. "You can see it acting up even through my shirt."

Grandma took one look and burst into tears. "Oh, Lem," she sobbed, "we've had such a good life together."

Just then Johnny, the six-year-old grandson, ripped into the room like a tornado. "I want my frog, Grandpa!" he cried.

"Your frog, Johnny?" questioned Grandpa. "I don't know anything about your frog!"

"It's in your shirt pocket, Grandpa," said Johnny. "I put it there this morning."

Grandpa looked at the boy for a moment, then reached into his shirt pocket. His face brightened, then broke into a broad grin. "So *that's* what's been thumpin' and jumpin' and actin' up!" he said. "Did you hear that, Ma?" he half shouted. "It's not my heart at all. It's just this ornery little frog! Here, take your frog, boy, and get out of here," he said as he tousled Johnny's hair.

Grandma dried her tears, laughed and hugged Grandpa all at the same time. "Bless that frog, bless that frog!" she said over and over.

"I ought to kill the ornery little rascal," Grandpa snorted. "He sure heaped a lot of work on my shoulders." He scratched his chin for a moment. "And about Milt Huggins," he said slowly. "We'll just feed him some other time."

Ewart A. Autry

Ewart A. Autry never lost sight of his Mississippi roots. Though he was busy pastoring rural churches in the South, he somehow found time to write for such publications as the *Reader's Digest, Better Homes & Gardens,* and *Field and Stream.* Among his books are *Ghost Hound of Thunder Valley* (1965), *Don't Look Back, Mama* (1979), and *In Prison . . . and Visited Me* (1952). Most of his writing occurred during mid and late twentieth century.

AN OLD-FASHIONED LOVE STORY

Betty Steele Everett

Two men were in love with her, but she just didn't know which one to choose—so she asked her great-grandmother.

Spring always reminds me of my great-grandmother and the year I was twenty-two. Gram was almost ninety then, and living in a nursing home because she had to be in a wheelchair. She still had a sense of humor, though, saying she'd be racing that chair in the Indy 500 someday. I told her she'd probably win, too!

That spring was a time of decision for me. I had been dating two men—Jerry Fulton and "Mac" McGinnis. Each knew about the other, but each was pressuring me to choose him and make it permanent with an engagement ring.

While visiting Gram one day, I explained the situation. "I like them both a lot, Gram, and I could love either one of them. They're both kind and good and fun to be with. Both have their careers mapped out. So I don't know which one to choose—or whether to stop dating both of them."

Gram smiled. "It's a problem a lot of girls would like."

"But what do *you* think about them, Gram? You've lived so long and know so much about people. Which one do you think I should stop seeing?"

Gram laid a hand on mine. "Amy, I'm an old woman. I can't make a decision for you. I like both men. But why don't you bring them to see me again?"

I had taken Jerry and Mac to see Gram before. Both had been polite, but also obviously relieved, when they left, to be out of the nursing home with its odors and noises and reminders of death.

Jerry went with me to see Gram the next Saturday. We talked about general things for a while, and then Gram began telling Jerry how she had met my great-grandfather.

"It was at a church picnic," she said, and her pale blue eyes got a faraway look in them. "He was new in town and had no one to eat with. Later he went into the woods and came back with a huge bunch of violets he had picked. He said they were for me, to thank me for being kind to a lonely stranger. And that was the beginning.

"He always brought me violets on the anniversary of that day," she said. "I had a pale blue vase I always put them in. I never used it for anything else. I suppose that sounds like an old-fashioned love story to you young people, but it will be seventy years a week from tomorrow."

The next day I brought Mac to see Gram. Before we left, she told him the same story about the violets.

I forgot about the story until the next Sunday when I went to see Gram alone. I was anxious to ask her what I should do. It wasn't fair to go on this way.

When I got to Gram's room, there was a beautiful arrangement of violets on her bedside table. The card, with the name of the largest florist in town, read, "From Jerry—to help you remember."

"Gram, Jerry sent violets! Like Gramps would have done! Wasn't that sweet? They must have cost a lot!"

She nodded. "They're beautiful. It was nice of him to remember my story."

I was sitting beside her wheelchair, trying to decide how to ask her what she thought of Jerry and Mac, when I heard footsteps in the corridor. Then Mac was standing in the doorway, looking surprised to see me.

"Why are you here?" I was surprised to see him, too.

Mac came into the room slowly, his hands behind his back. "I brought something for you, Gram. You told us when we were here the other day . . ." Suddenly he stopped, looking at the violets on the table. "Oh, I see someone has—I mean, I didn't know. . . ."

"What do you have?" I asked. "Come on, show us."

"Nothing." Mac was backing out of the room.

Gram leaned forward in her wheelchair. "You brought me something, young man, and I want to see it. I can follow you wherever you go, in this chair, so you might as well show me. Did you bring me violets?"

Mac nodded. "But it—now it's not—you already have . . ." He brought his hands around so we could see the large bunch of violets. He had put them in a pale blue vase, but beside the professionally arranged ones they looked like what a child might offer.

I didn't know what to say. I felt sorry for Mac and Gram both, and embarrassed for us all. If Gram had only allowed Mac to leave and get rid of the flowers. . . .

But Gram took the violets and buried her face in them. "Oh, Mac, thank you! You picked them yourself, didn't you? And found the right vase. . . . They look and smell just like the ones Joseph used to bring me!"

She was crying, and I could only stare at her. The perfectly arranged ones from Jerry had not had this effect on her! And suddenly I understood why. Jerry had given to her of his money, but Mac had given of his time and energy to pick the violets, find the vase he thought would be most like the one Gram remembered, and bring them to her himself. He had been willing to do all that to make an old woman happy.

Gram has been gone many years now, but she lived to see Mac and me married, to see our first child, and to see the pictures of the woods behind our home.

I hear Mac coming from the woods now. I have the vase all ready for half the violets he will be bringing. I guess you could call ours an old-fashioned love story, too. I realize now that Gram used the story of the violets to show me something about both Jerry and Mac, and we will have violets in the house as long as they last.

The other half of what Mac has picked? Those we'll take to the cemetery this afternoon. Gram's grave always looks nicer with fresh and lovely spring violets on it.

Betty Steele Everett

Betty Steele Everett wrote for popular magazines during the second half of the twentieth century.

A GIFT FOR LAUREN

Denise Anderson Boiko

What should he give her—what could he, with so little money—for her sixteenth birthday? This granddaughter whom he loved with his very soul. This granddaughter who was almost a carbon copy of another oh-so-special girl long ago.

Philip rose stiffly from the bench as he saw the bus approaching. The cold November wind whipped across his face, and his achy joints rebelled as he straightened up and shuffled toward the curb to mount the bus headed for the shopping mall. Today was his last chance to buy Lauren a gift before her birthday celebration tomorrow. He had procrastinated too long already. Not because he didn't want to buy her a gift. Certainly not. Lauren was the light of his life, and the thought of presenting her with something special brought him great joy.

No, the problem was simply that he had not been able to think of the right gift for her this year. Tomorrow Lauren, his only grandchild, turned sixteen. In her childhood years, it had been easy enough to find a toy to delight her already-sunny personality. As she grew older, he had commemorated her birthday by saving a few dollars from his meager income to give her a dollar for every year of her age.

But this year had to be different. A girl's sixteenth birthday was a momentous occasion. A gift for Lauren's sixteenth birthday had to be the most memorable one yet. It must be something she would treasure for years to come—something that symbolized the beauty of the young woman she was becoming.

As the bus stormed off down the crowded city street, Philip closed his eyes for a moment and smiled as the image of Lauren came to his mind. He did not need to refer to the many photos of her in his wallet to recall her face. The child seemed to have been born beaming with delight and sharing that delight with others. Her dark wavy hair and her soft but sparkling brown eyes, together with her quick, radiant smile, were only part of her beauty. Lauren possessed an unusual sensitivity to people's feelings, and she had especially won the heart of this old wrinkled grandpa. She always had a special hug and kiss for "Grandpa Philip" and never grew tired of listening to him tell of his young years with his wife, Laura, for whom Lauren was named.

Thinking of Laura now, his trembling hand reached into his coat pocket for a small but thick leather-bound volume. He ran his hand lovingly over its worn chestnut-colored cover and flipped through page after page of Laura's tiny, neat handwriting. Opening it to the first page, he read once again the familiar words.

> *April 30, 1939*
> *It is my sixteenth birthday, and what wonderful gifts I have received! First of all, this leather-bound diary. How did Mama and Papa know that I had been longing for a place to record my thoughts and dreams? I plan to faithfully fill this book, not only with the details of my days and weeks and months, but also (especially!) with what I am feeling. Now that I am practically grown up (after all, I will finish high school in just a little over a year), there are so many things I think about day after day. Sometimes I think I will go crazy if I don't have anyone to share them with. I think keeping a diary will help tremendously.*
>
> *But back to the gifts. Another beautiful gift was the string of sky-blue beads from Uncle Mark and Aunt Esther. They are simply the loveliest beads I have ever seen. Not to be vain (for Mama always reminds me that true beauty comes from within), but I do think that these beads will look stunning with my white summer dress.*
>
> *And to make my delight even more complete, Mama and Papa also gave me a splendid drawing set with colored pencils, pastel crayons, and charcoal pencils, all packed in a lovely wooden case. It's like a small suitcase. Now I can go out to the woods to sketch, and come home with beautiful colored masterpieces.*

I feel so fortunate to be able to celebrate my birthday in such a lavish way. After all, so many people have little or no money just now. Many of my friends' fathers have lost their jobs and even their homes and properties. I'm grateful (as Mama always reminds me I should be) that we still have a home and a little money set aside. I know I shall make the very best use of these thoughtful birthday presents. I will remember them always. This has been the best sixteenth birthday a girl could ever have!

Philip looked up and sighed. Placing the diary tenderly back into his pocket, he withdrew his wallet and carefully counted out its contents. Perhaps he had a bill or two tucked away which he had previously overlooked. No, the total was just as he had expected: twenty-six dollars and thirty-five cents. And part of that had to go for bus fare for the trip home. He patted his other pocket where half a peanut butter sandwich on a rather dry piece of bread resided. Accumulating the twenty-six dollars for Lauren's gift had not been an easy task. It had meant skipping a meal here, turning the furnace down a few more degrees there, putting off getting new shoes, and making other little sacrifices. Lauren was worth every bit of it, and more. But even so, he feared that twenty-six dollars would not go far at the Brookmont Shopping Towne.

As the bus pulled up at the shopping center, he disembarked, carefully clutching the handrail and turning around to thank the bus driver. The bus zoomed away in a cloud of exhaust, and he stood, disoriented for a moment, gazing at the mass of humanity heading into the mall for their Saturday shopping.

Slowly, deliberately, he made his way to the first department store and stopped at the jewelry counter. He examined the trinkets on display, discouraged by the price tags and also by the cheap appearance of the items. Sales clerks punched buttons on their cash registers; customers pawed through racks of pins and earrings and strings of beads. He searched and searched but did not see what he was looking for. Stepping over to the corner of the counter, he tried to catch the sales clerks' eye. No one seemed to notice him.

"Miss?" he called hesitantly as one of the clerks rushed past. Glancing at him, she replied, "I'll be with you in a moment." After waiting several minutes, he was finally rewarded by her appearance opposite the counter from him. "May I help you?" she asked, glancing at her watch.

"I was looking for . . . actually, I was wondering. . . . Do you have any—ah—sky-blue beads?"

"Any what?" asked the clerk, then interrupted herself as her supervisor came by, "Lucy, it's time for my break. Can I go?"

"Right after you've finished with this customer," Lucy responded.

The clerk turned back. "Now what was it you were looking for?"

"Well, I was wondering if you had any sky blue beads."

"Sky blue? What kind of stone?"

"Ah—I'm not exactly sure. Just sky blue."

She sighed. "Well, I don't think we have any sky-blue beads, but here are some nice turquoise beads." She pulled a string of beads from a rack and displayed them on the counter.

He gazed at them, as the clerk drummed her fingers on the glass countertop. They were pretty enough. Turquoise would look lovely on Lauren. But they weren't sky blue. He'd have to think about it.

Philip looked up at the clerk "How much do they cost, miss?"

She lifted a small white tag and read, "Twenty-nine ninety-nine. Shall I ring them up for you?"

His heart sank. "Well, I'll have to think about it. Thank you kindly, miss."

He stumbled off into the mall, into the sea of people and the sea of stores. How he wished he could just say glibly, "I'll take it" and have her ring up those turquoise beads. But they weren't sky blue, and even worse, they cost more than he'd managed to scrape up.

Sitting on a bench to rest his joints again, he pulled out the leather diary and flipped it open to the middle. Turning a few pages, he found another well-worn entry. This was his favorite part.

> *August 20, 1940*
> *I have met a delightful young man named Philip, and we get along marvelously. He is the son of one of Papa's friends, and I met him when our family was invited to dinner at their home tonight. Philip is twenty-two years old (four years older than I), and we spent the whole evening conversing and laughing—especially laughing. We discovered that we both like historical books, cinnamon toast, roses, and musical theater. We poked fun at things we don't like: modern art, snobby little dogs dressed in sweaters, and on and on. He is in the Army in officers' training. How fortunate that the U.S. is not involved in this awful world war. I want to be able to see Philip as much as possible.*

He leaned back and closed his eyes. How well he remembered the night when he and Laura had met. Even without the prompting of her diary, that August evening sixty years ago could have been yesterday. He had known as soon as he heard her sweet laughter, which contrasted intriguingly with the sincere, thoughtful look in her eyes, that this young woman was someone he had to get to know better.

And now young Lauren had those same eyes. Sparkling brown eyes that could dance with fun and humor, yet soften in sympathetic understanding over someone's troubles—even if that someone were only a wrinkled little grandpa.

Flipping a few pages further along in the diary, he found another familiar entry. This one was adorned with a bit of lace and a white satin ribbon.

January 16, 1942
Today I will join many of my agemates in the role of War Bride. Pearl Harbor has, for Philip and I, as well as many others, hastened the wearing of wedding pearls. My head is still whirling with all that has happened in the past month. Mama is a miracle worker to have prepared for this wedding in just a few short weeks, as soon as we knew Philip would definitely be going overseas. I've glued a bit of the "makings" of my wedding dress onto this page as a remembrance of this day I'll never forget. It is still early in the morning, but I am so ready to stand next to my beloved Philip and say "I do . . ." for better or worse. Unfortunately, with this war, there is no guarantee of "better," but I will try not to think about that on this glorious day. Whatever happens, I will have the joy of knowing that I am Philip's and he is mine as long as we both shall live. And when this war is over, we will have our own little home and some miniature Philips and Lauras to fill our home with laughter and love!

Philip smiled as he remembered their wedding ceremony in the little community church. Midway through the ceremony,

Laura's high-heeled shoe had gotten caught on the hem of her dress and in trying to free it, Laura ended up with the giggles. She didn't exactly break out in laughter, but her eyes were dancing and she was taking deep breaths to keep her mirth under control. But just a few moments later, as the minister had them join hands to repeat their vows, those same eyes had filled with tears as she had looked up at Philip with an expression of love and commitment that he could never forget. "With all my heart," she had added in a choked voice after her fervent "I do," and Philip's eyes, too, had filled with tears. How could he go off to war and leave this precious companion?

It constantly amazed Philip how much Lauren was like her grandmother. They had never met, of course. How he wished they had! They would have made a charming pair. How Laura would have fussed over her and fixed her up. She had always wanted a little girl and a little boy, to begin with. Then, as she had said merrily many times, "The rest can be anything. Up to ten, would you say, Philip, dear? Then we'll stop and just enjoy them till they grow up."

She did have her little boy. That was their son James, Lauren's father. How delighted they had both been with his birth! Misty-eyed, Philip turned the pages of the journal until he came to the entry.

May 2, 1944
I write with tears of joy streaming down my face. Our darling little son, James Lawrence, was born yesterday. How I wish Philip had been here with me! I know I must be patriotic and think about my country—and all the countries of the world for which our men are fighting. He will be here soon enough when he earns his next leave. But until then I will delight myself with gazing at my beautiful

son, brushing his soft cheek with my fingertips, and thanking God for this miracle. I wish for many, many more! What could be more wonderful than raising a whole family of precious boys and girls with my beloved Philip, and watching them grow up into young men and women we can be proud of? I am too overcome with joy and awe to find words to describe what I'm feeling. I can hardly wait until Philip is home again and we can be reunited as a family. I love that word: FAMILY.

He stood up and stretched, glancing at the clock in the shopping mall. It was time to continue the search for Lauren's gift. Perhaps an art set like the one Laura had received would be an appropriate gift. Making his way toward an art and hobby store, he politely inquired of the clerk, "Would you happen to have any sets of art supplies in wooden carrying cases?"

"Oh, yes, sir. Right this way." The clerk indicated the display, and Philip gazed at them one by one. Checking the price tags was once again a disheartening experience. Fifty-five dollars for a beautiful set with pastel crayons, charcoal and colored pencils, watercolor paints, and six different brushes. Forty-five dollars for a similar set minus the pastels. Thirty dollars for a set of watercolors and brushes. For only fifteen dollars, he could get an assortment of colored and charcoal pencils in a carrying case. That might be a possibility, but somehow it didn't seem worthy of Lauren's sixteenth birthday.

The clerk stood, expectantly, waiting for his decision.

"I . . . thank you so much for showing these to me. You have been so kind. I will have to think about it for a little while."

The clerk nodded and returned to the cash register.

Philip, suddenly weary, slipped out of the store and sank onto the nearest bench. Pulling his peanut butter sandwich out of his pocket, he began to take small nibbles while he thought:

What could he give Lauren for this once-in-a-lifetime birthday? She was worth a very grand gift, but what could a poor grandpa with a limited budget find for her?

After finishing his sandwich and carefully wiping his fingertips off on his handkerchief, he once again opened the diary. He skimmed through the pages, reliving the joy of his and Laura's reunion after the war. He half read, half remembered, their walks in the park with little James toddling along beside them. He remembered how they had fed the ducks and how James had roared with laughter each time the ducks grabbed the bits of bread—and how he'd howled with outraged surprise and pain when one of them nipped the chubby fingers which held the bread.

Golden days, beautiful days. Days of happiness as a family. Philip and Laura and James. With a bittersweet smile, he read the entry from the fall of 1947.

> *October 20, 1947*
> *What a beautiful autumn it is! The leaves have turned their delightful colors, and James loves to chase them and collect them as the breeze blows them around. I am not very adept at chasing leaves or toddlers, however. This new baby will be born in just two months, more or less. Of course, I am hoping for less. It is not easy to care for James while being so large and so tired! But Philip and I are filled with joy. Baby number two will be loved and cuddled and so very welcome in our home. Oh, how I hope for a daughter! Then, as I still tell Philip, the next eight can be anything! We are looking for a bigger house for our growing family. How glad I am that the war is over and life is getting back to normal. I have never been more perfectly happy than I am now. God has blessed us unbelievably, and I thank Him every day for what He has done.*

The diary entries ended there. Taking out his handkerchief, Philip dabbed at his eyes, once more remembering that autumn, more than fifty years ago. Just two days after she had written that entry, Laura's labor had suddenly started and she had become very ill. Their tiny daughter, Elizabeth Anne, had come into the world but was too small and too young to live for more than a few hours. Laura had held her briefly, and Philip could still picture that look of joy and love mixed with pain that had filled his wife's face during those minutes. But all too soon, baby Elizabeth slipped away—and that night Laura did, too. The doctor had gently broken the news to Philip, who had known immediately that his life would never be the same again.

The years had passed surprisingly quickly, and as a single father, Philip had done his best to make sure James knew how deeply he was loved. After a succession of housekeepers, he had finally discovered Trina, a middle-aged "grandma" type who fussed over James and baked him cookies and made him laugh with her half-fact, half-fiction stories of her childhood in the "Old Country." Trina, the matchmaker, was constantly trying to pair Philip with this or that lady from church or from the neighborhood or from the Women's Club. But Philip knew his heart would always belong to Laura. He was content to watch his son grow up, and he took comfort from the fact that James was developing into a steady, responsible young man, devoted to his father.

James went off to college and then was admitted into law school. He was a serious student and did well for himself. So dedicated was he to his work that he was well into his thirties before he realized that he should think about marriage. But when he had met Lynn, a fellow attorney, he pursued courtship with the same serious determination that had gained him his education and career. They married just a few months later, and after four years of difficulties in having a child, they presented Grandpa Philip with little Lauren.

And now as he contemplated her sixteenth birthday gift and realized that time was running out, he was at a loss. How could he arrive at Lauren's party empty-handed, or with some common, token gift? She had given him so much by her generous, friendly disposition. She deserved the best—something she could treasure for many years, if not the rest of her life. Something, perhaps, that she could keep to remember him after he was gone.

Suddenly Philip knew. He leaped off the bench—at least, he came as close to leaping as he could with his stiff joints. He headed purposefully toward a shop in the middle of the mall, made a quick purchase, and, with a package clutched under his arm, pulled his thin coat more tightly around him as he exited to the chilly outdoors and made his way back to the bus stop.

Back home, he arranged the gift in a white box and lovingly tied it with a bit of gold ribbon saved from a previous package. Feeling exhausted, he heated a can of soup, ate quickly, and settled wearily into bed.

On Sunday afternoon, Philip took the bus to the stop nearest his son's house. Lynn had offered to come pick him up, but he had preferred to find his own transportation and enjoy some moments alone to anticipate Lauren's reaction to his gift.

"Grandpa Philip!" Before he even entered the house, he was surrounded by Lauren's young, strong arms, and had a light kiss planted on his cheek. "Come in and have a seat. All my friends are here and we're playing some games." She led him by the hand and he spent an enjoyable hour conversing with James and Lynn and watching the young people playing silly games.

Soon the birthday cake was served. Seating him at the head of the table, as she always enjoyed doing, Lauren gazed at him with a loving smile. Her brown eyes sparkled more than ever in the candlelight and in the excitement of the day. She was wearing a rose-colored dress today, and even had roses in her hair. Sitting nearby, her girlfriends clamored for attention and made bantering comments about this or that.

Lauren blew out every one of the sixteen candles, and busily jumped up to begin cutting the cake and handing it out. "Grandpa first!" she announced as she presented him with a piece of German chocolate cake, which happened to be both his favorite and her favorite. Philip savored his cake, but also cherished the cheerful scene around him: the table full of colorful gifts, Lauren's bright face beaming, James and Lynn watching the festivities in their quiet, pleasant way. *How Laura would have loved this,* he thought to himself with a smile. *She would have been right there in the midst of it, trying to force extra helpings of cake on the guests.*

Finally it was time to open gifts. Lauren oohed and aahed over bracelets, earrings, a handbag, a sweater or two, gift certificates from her parents. Philip held his gift aside so it would be opened last. When he handed it to her, hands trembling, she looked at him with those expressive eyes and said, "I know I'll love whatever is in here, Grandpa."

Her friend Jessie, who had been making joking comments about some of the gifts, peered over Lauren's shoulder as she untied the gold ribbon and carefully lifted the lid of the white box. As Lauren brushed the covering of tissue paper aside, Jessie leaned over and said, "Oh, an old book. How boring." Lauren's face was hidden as she looked down at the book. She opened it slowly and flipped through it, but didn't say a word.

He waited, almost without breathing, for her reaction. But it was a long time in coming. She continued to turn page after page, as though looking for clues to the identity of the writer.

Then, as she turned to the front page, her eyes lit up as she recognized the name and date written there.

But even now she did not forget her role as hostess: she turned to her friends smilingly and said, "Please forgive me if I leave you for a while. There's something in these pages that can't wait!" Then she turned to that first entry. And the second. And on and on . . . until she came to the end.

She sat still for what seemed to her grandfather to be forever, so long did it seem. *What is she thinking?* he wondered. Was it a mistake to have given her this diary? Should he have waited until she was older? He tried in vain to read her face, but her eyes were staring somewhere far away.

Finally, she stood, and turned towards him, and he could see that her face was wet with tears. He stood, and she came into his arms, still crying. His aged heart thumping so loudly he felt everyone in the room could hear it, he just continued to hold her tenderly.

He sighed with a sense of supreme happiness. His gift had been accepted as the greatest gift in all the world. The gift of her past.

Denise Anderson Boiko

Denise Anderson Boiko, a freelance writer, today lives in San Jose, California.

A H

THE MASON FAMILY ON EXHIBITION

Author Unknown

Katherine made sure her rowdy family understood her ultimatum: Everybody was to be on their very best behavior for Professor Baldridge's momentous visit. But she hadn't known that someone from her past would choose that day to make an unannounced visit.

The Mason household was to entertain company for dinner. That in itself was nothing unusual, but on this coming day it was the guest-to-be himself who was out of the ordinary.

Specifically, he was to be Katherine's company, but the family had been cautioned by Mother that they were by no manner of means to refer to him as Katherine's acquisition. Katherine was the eldest Mason daughter, serious-eyed, lithe, lovely—just graduated from the state university.

The coming guest was Keith Baldridge, assistant professor of history at Katherine's alma mater. He was thirty-two and unmarried. No, he was not Katherine's fiancé—Katherine's manner dared anyone to suggest it. As a matter of fact, their friendship was at that very delicate stage where the least breath might shrivel the emerging chrysalis, or blow it into a gorgeous-winged creature of love.

In the meantime, it was going to be an awful strain on the family to have him come. Mother was already feeling the effects of Katherine's attempts to make over the entire family in the few days intervening before his arrival.

"How long's Professor Baldhead—I can't think of his real name—going to stay?" Junior wanted to know at the supper table, in the middle of the week. Junior was twelve.

"There he goes, Mamma," Katherine said, plaintively. "Can't you keep him from saying those horrid things?"

"My son," Father addressed him from the head of the table, "have you never heard of the children in the Bible who were eaten by bears when they said, 'Go up, thou baldhead'?" Junior grinned appreciatively, realizing he was not being very violently reproved.

"If you could just know, Mamma, how different the Baldridge

home is from ours!" Katherine was in the kitchen now, assisting Mother and Tillie. "Our family is so talkative and noisy, and laughs over every little silly thing, and there is so much confusion. Why, at their dinners—besides Professor Baldridge there's just his father and an aunt, both so aristocratic—at their dinners it's so quiet and the conversation is so *enlightening*—about Rodin, and—Wagner—and, oh, maybe Milton's "Il Penseroso"—you know what I mean—so much more *refined.*

"And I wish you could *see* their house. It's not as big as ours, and really no nicer, but oh! The *atmosphere!* The hangings are gray or mauve or dark purple—and they keep the shades down so much lower than ours—so it's peaceful, you know, like twilight all the time."

"My! Ain't that a gloomy way to live, and unhealthful, too, I must say." It was Tillie, speaking acridly.

Tillie's status in the Mason family might as well be inserted here. She was an old maid who had gone to country school with Mother when Mother was Molly Warner. Unlike Mother, who had gone to college, Tillie's schooling had ended with the fifth reader. For eighteen years she had been in the household, as much a part of it as Father or the kitchen sink. Homely, ungainly, she worked like a horse for them all, or "slicked up" and went comfortably downtown or to missionary meeting with Mother. No, the servant problem had never worried Mother.

So now, with the familiarity which comes from having braided a little girl's hair and officiated at the pulling of her first tooth, Tillie was speaking her mind.

Katherine continued.

"And pictures! Why folks, in one room there's just *one,* a dull, dim, old wood scene, and so artistic. You can imagine how Papa's bank calendar in our dining-room just makes me *sick.* And they have a Japanese servant. You never hear him coming, but suddenly he's right there at your elbow, so quiet and—"

"*My!* How spooky!"

"Oh, Tillie, *no!* It's the most exquisite service you ever saw—to have him gliding in and out and anticipating your every wish."

"Well, Kathie, I'll wait table for you, and glad to, but I ain't goin' to do no slippin' around like a heathen, I can promise you that."

"Thank you, Tillie; and Tillie, when you pass things to him, please don't say anything to him, he's so used to that unobtrusive kind of being waited on—and he's so quiet and reserved himself."

"Well, if I had a glum man like that, I'd teach him a few things."

At that, Katherine left the kitchen with dignity, which gave Tillie a chance to say, "I declare, she riles me so this week!" To which Mother replied, "Don't be too hard on her, Tillie. It's exasperating, I know; but she's nervous."

Mother was worried, too. She had never seen Keith Baldridge, and numerous questions of doubt filled her mind. What manner of man was this that lived in a house of perpetual twilight!

The family managed to live through Tuesday, Wednesday, and Thursday. The word Friday seemed to have a portentous meaning, as if it were the day set apart for a cyclone, or something was to happen to the sun.

It came—Friday. To the Mason family it was *The Day*. It proved to be a still, hot morning, full of humidity and the buzzing and bumbling of insects.

At the breakfast table Katherine gave the last of her multitudinous directions. "Mamma, I wish you'd *muzzle* Junior. Make him promise not to *open* his mouth."

"My child—" Mother's tone signified that it was making its last patient stand—"Junior shall be the pink of propriety, I assure you."

After breakfast Katherine went upstairs to dress. Then for some time she sat waiting, starting up at the sound of every car. Then she saw someone turning in at the front walk. He was short and slightly stooped. He carried a cane, but seemed to hobble along without using it. He wore store clothes too large for him, and a black, wide-brimmed felt hat over his white hair. It was Grandpa, Grandpa Warner, who lived with another daughter on his old home farm, and had evidently come to surprise Mother's family.

Katherine started up with a cry. "Not that! Oh, not Grandpa—*today!*" It was too cruel! Why, Grandpa monopolized conversation with his reminiscences, and at the table he did unspeakable things with his knife.

The good fairy which is called Memory reminded Katherine of the days when she had slipped her hand into Grandpa's and gone skipping along with him through dewy, honey-sweet clover to drive the cows down to the lower pasture; days when she had snuggled down by him in the old homemade sleigh and been whirled through an elf land of snow-covered trees and ice-locked rivulets; days that then seemed to embody to her all the happiness that time could hold. But she turned away from the wistful fairy, and looked bitterly out upon a day that was unconditionally spoiled.

Carrying herself reluctantly downstairs, she perfunctorily greeted the old man. Mother, a happy moisture in her eyes, was making a great fuss over him. Temporarily she had forgotten that such a personage as Keith Baldridge existed.

Back in a few moments to her room, Katherine continued her watchful waiting.

A car turned in at the driveway, a long, low, gray car, and Keith Baldridge, in ulster and auto cap, stepped out. Katherine went to meet him.

As for Mother, as Keith Baldridge grasped her hand, her own heart dropped from something like ninety beats a minute to its normal seventy-two. He was big and athletic-looking, and under well-modeled brows shone gray-blue eyes that were unmistakably frank and kind. With that God-given intuition of mothers, she knew that he was *clean*—clean in mind and soul and body. She would do everything in her power to make his stay pleasant and to follow out Katherine's desires.

So she hurried to the kitchen to see that everything was just as she knew Katherine wanted it. She saw that the crushed fruit was chilled, that the salad was crisp, the baked potatoes were piping hot. The long table looked lovely, she admitted. Just before she called them in, Mother pulled the shades down part way, so that the room seemed "peaceful—you know, like twilight."

They all came trooping in, Father continuing what he had evidently begun on the porch, a cheerful monologue on the income tax law. Bob and Mabel, who had arrived with the new baby in the Reed cab[7] that Father Mason had given them, held a prolonged discussion as to where the cab and its wonderful contents could most safely stand during dinner.

With that old-fashioned notion that men folks like to talk together, Mother placed Keith Baldridge and Bob and Grandpa up at the end of the table by Father.

As they were being seated, Father said in that sprightly way which always came to him when a royal repast confronted him: "What's the matter with the curtains?" Then, walking over to the window, with the highly original remark, "Let's have more light

[7] *Probably a bassinet.*

on the subject," he snapped the shades up to the limit. Mother felt like throttling Father, but of course she couldn't just get up and jerk the shades down again.

Tillie, with an exaggerated tiptoeing around the table, began passing the plates as Father served them.

There was a little interval of silence as the dinner started, then Grandpa looked down the table toward Katherine, and said in his old, cracked voice, "Well, Tattern!" It was her childish nickname, put away on the shelf with her dolls and dishes. It sounded silly today. "What you goin' to do with yourself now you've graduated?"

"I'm going to teach in the Miles City High School, Grandfather."

"What you goin' to teach?"

"History," she said briefly.

"Then git married, I s'pose, and have no more use fer your history? That makes me think of somethin' that happened back in Illynois. It was a big thing fer anybody from our neck of the woods to go to college, but Abner Hoskins went, and when he was 'most through he got drowned. At the funeral Mrs. Stearns walked round the casket and looked at the corpse 'n' said, 'My! My! What a lot o' good learnin' gone to waste.' "

Everyone laughed. Katherine's own contribution to the general hubbub was of a sickly, artificial variety.

"You came here from Illinois at an early date, I suppose, Mr. Warner?" Keith Baldridge asked.

It was like a match to dynamite—no, like a match to a straw stack, a damp straw stack that would burn all afternoon. Grandpa looked as pleased as a little boy.

"Yes, sir—it was 1865. I fought with the old Illynois boys first, and then I loaded up and came, with teams, of course. That was a great trip, that was. Yes, sir! I mind, fer instance, how we crossed a crick, and comin' down a steep bank, the wagon tipped over, 'n' our flour—there was eight sacks—spilled in the water. Well, sir, would you believe them sacks of flour wasn't harmed, we got 'em out so quick? The water 'n' flour made a thin paste on the outside 'n' the rest wasn't hurt. I rec'lect the youngsters runnin' down the crick after Ma's good goose feather pillows that was floatin' 'way."

Two scarlet spots burned on Katherine's cheeks. She raised miserable eyes, which had been fixed steadily upon her plate, to see Keith Baldridge looking at Grandpa in amazement. What was he thinking? Comparing Grandpa with his own father, dignified and scholarly?

On and on went Grandpa. "Yes, sir—the year I'm tellin' you about was the year the grasshoppers came, 1874.

"They came in the fall, you know, 'n' et the corn, 'n' then they had the gall to stay all winter 'n' hatch in the spring. Why, there wasn't nothin' raised in the gardens that summer but pieplant 'n' tomatoes. Them two things. Yes, sir, me 'n' Ma had the first sod house in Otre County. 'N' poor! Why, Job's turkey belonged in Rockefeller's flock by the side o' us. I had one coat, 'n' Ma had one dress fer I don't know how long, 'n' Molly over there—" he pointed with his knife to Mother, who smiled placidly back— "Molly had a little dress made outen flour sacks. The brand of flour had been called Hellas. Ma got the words all outen the dress but the first four letters of the brand, 'n' there it was right across Molly's back, 'H-E-L-L,' 'n' Ma had to make some kind of knittin' trimmin' to cover it up."

Everyone laughed hilariously, Mother most of all. Junior shouted as if he were in a grandstand. Katherine gave a very good imitation of a lady laughing while taking a tablespoonful of castor oil.

Oh, it was awful! What would he think? He was laughing—but of course he would laugh! He was the personification of courtesy and tact.

The dinner was over. Father, with the same nonchalance that he would have displayed had he been dining with cabinet members, walked coolly into the library, and with the automobile section of the paper over his face, prepared to take his afternoon nap.

Katherine, unceremoniously leaving Mr. Baldridge to the rest of the family, slipped out to the kitchen to wipe dishes for Mother and Tillie.

"Why, Kathie, you go right back!" Mother insisted.

"Let me be, please," she said irritably. "I know what I want to do."

Mother, giving her oldest daughter a swift look, had a desire to take her across her knee and spank her, even as in days of yore.

The work done, Katherine walked slowly up the back stairs, bathed her flushed face, and with a feeling that life held nothing worthwhile, went down to join the family. As she surveyed the scene from the vestibule it seemed to her it couldn't have been worse.

Grandpa, for Keith Baldridge's benefit, was elaborating on the never-ending subject of grasshoppers. As he paused, Tillie, in her best black silk, came around the corner of the porch and sat down near the guest, with "Be you any relation to the Baldridges down in East Suffolk, Connecticut?" *(Oh, what would he think of Tillie, who had waited on him, doing that?)* Junior, on the other side of Mr. Baldridge, was making frantic attempts to show him a disgusting eel in an old fish globe that was half full of slimy green water. Even the Maltese cat was croqueting herself in and out through Professor Baldridge's legs. To Katherine's super sensitive state of mind, the confusion was as if all bedlam had broken out.

With a feeling of numb indifference, she stepped out on the porch. Keith Baldridge rose nimbly to his feet. "Now, good people," he said, pleasantly, apparently unabashed, "I'm going to take Miss Katherine away for a while in the car. You'll all be here, will you, when I get back?"

Katherine got into her auto things and went down the steps with him, no joy in her heart—nothing but a sense of playing her part callously in a scene that would soon end.

"I'm certainly elated over the find I made today," said Mr. Baldridge.

"Find?" Katherine questioned politely.

"Yes—your grandfather. He's a wonderful man! He's promised to come to my home next week and stay several days with me. He's just what I've been looking for: an intelligent man who has lived through the early history of the state and whose memory is so keen that he can recall hundreds of anecdotes. I am working on a history of the state, and my plan is to have it contain stories of vividness and color. From the moment he began to talk I realized what a gold mine I had struck. I could scarcely refrain from having a pad and pencil in my hand all the time I was listening to him. Why, he's a great character—one of the typical pathfinders—sturdy, honorable, and lovable. You must be proud of him.

"I'm a crank on the subject of these old pioneers," he went on. "To me they were the bravest, the most wonderful people in the world. Look at the scene before us. Think of it! To have changed an immense area of Indian-inhabited wild land into this! Visualize to yourself, in place of what you see, a far-reaching stretch of prairie land on every side of us, with only the wild grass rippling over it. Now imagine this: You and I are standing here alone in the midst of it, with nothing but a prairie schooner containing a few meager necessities by our side. We're here to stay. From this same prairie we must build our home with our hands, wrest our food, adequately clothe ourselves. It is to be a battle. We must conquer or be conquered. Would you have had the courage to do that?" He turned to her with his fine, frank smile. And into Katherine Mason's heart came the swift, bittersweet knowledge that she could have made sod houses and delved in the earth for food and killed wild animals for clothing—with Keith Baldridge.

"And this," he went on again, indicating the landscape, "this is our heritage from the pioneers. From sod houses to such beautiful homes as yours! I can't tell you how much I've enjoyed being in your family today. When I think of my own gloomy boyhood, I could fight someone—a lonesome, motherless little tad studying manners and 'Thanatopsis' under a tutor. Yours is the kind of home I've always wanted. It's the kind of home I mean to have when—if—I marry—all sunshine—and laughter."

It was late afternoon when the long gray car turned into the Mason driveway and stopped at the side lawn. In fact, it was so much later than Keith Baldridge had planned to leave that he only took time to run up to the porch to say good-by to them all. If he expected the Masons to sit calmly on the porch when he should drive away, he did not yet know the Masons. One and all, excepting Grandpa, who stayed in his rocker, followed him down the steps, flocking across the green, sloping lawn to where his car stood. The cat, seeing the entire family trooping in one direction, came bounding across the yard, tail in air, and rubbed herself against the departing guest's trousers.

They all shook hands with him a second time. He got into the car and pressed the button that gave life to the monster. The wheels seemed quivering to turn. Just then Grandpa rose from his chair on the porch and excitedly waved his cane. "Say!" he called. He came hobbling over the grass, the late summer sun touching his scraggly gray hair. "Wait a minute, Mr. Baldridge!"

They all turned to watch him apprehensively, he seemed so hurried and anxious. He was close to the family group now. "Say! Mr. Baldridge! I jes' happened to think of somethin' else about them grasshoppers!"

They all laughed—all but Katherine, for she was not there. She had slipped into the front door and up to her room. There she dropped on her knees by the side of her bed and made a fervent prayer to the God of families, that she might be purged from the sin of having been, even in thought, disloyal to her own.

ONE BREATH AWAY

Alfred J. Eckhardt

Few things strike more terror in the heart than having someone you love deeply be diagnosed with Alzheimer's disease. What if it was your grandmother? Who would take care of her?

Have you ever heard someone say of certain people, "They are of no possible use to anyone, so we don't need to keep them around—they'd be better off dead."

Such a one was my grandmother. She didn't measure up. By the best medical diagnosis and the world's yardstick, her life was not worthwhile. In 1982 she thought Eisenhower was the president of the United States; she thought that she was always in Karnes City, Texas, even though she had not lived there for years; she talked to lamps and chairs as if they were the most precious children you could ever hope to know; and she always set a place at the table (complete with beverage, food, knife, fork, and napkin) for her departed husband, who had been deceased for a number of years. She had Alzheimer's.

Things had not always been like this. She had been a hardworking country woman all her life. I remember hearing stories of her milking cows and scrubbing bottles on the dairy farm; and in her younger years how she had picked rows and rows of cotton for very little pay. I also remember a time sitting at her table when I asked her, "Where did this tablespoon that has 'U.S. Government' stamped on it come from?" She explained, "Your grandfather would go and get the big barrels of leftover scraps from the internment camp in Kennedy to slop the hogs with, and this is one of the spoons that had fallen into the wasted food barrel."

She taught me to drive on rarely used dirt roads when I was only nine and she, with the most sincere look of love in her eyes, would often tell me while I was growing up, "Now, little Buddy, use your head." Everywhere around her house were bottles and cans filled with bolts, nuts, screws, and other useful items. Everything was saved for future use; nothing was wasted.

I honestly think she spent most of each day cleaning. One year for Christmas we gave her a set of wooden canisters with roosters painted on them. By the next Christmas she had cleaned them so many times most of the design had been rubbed off. Every Sunday she would attend the Methodist church and would still be singing hymns on Monday as she went about her chores. She had two sons; my father was one and the other, my uncle Bill, had only lived for a day.

Now, late in her life, here she was boarding with other elderly ladies at the San Antonio home of a registered nurse. Meanwhile, God had been helping to prepare me for the next stage of my life. For some time I had been tiring of the routine of my life. It seemed as though I was going to work to make money to go to work to make money to go to work ad nauseam. I came to the conclusion that the only way I could lead a truly meaningful life was to serve God. At that time the only way I could serve God seemed to be by serving other people. Even though I had a college degree, I scoured the newspaper want ads for a job whereby I could put myself into God's service.

One day, I came across an advertisement for a cook at the Methodist Mission Home. Their mission is to aid unwed mothers and the deaf. I responded to the advertisement and was assured that most of their food was frozen and all one had to do was heat it. Perhaps this might be the answer to my quest. An interview was set up. Just as I was walking out the door, the phone rang. It was my dad. It seemed the lady taking care of my grandmother could no longer do so since she was in need of triple-bypass heart surgery. Dad asked me if I wanted to take care of Grandma. Or should he place her in a nursing home? At that exact moment I felt the Holy Spirit ask me a question: *If you can't help your own family, what makes you think you can help anyone else?* With that thought in mind I told my dad I would accept the responsibility. That choice changed my life completely for the next fifteen years.

I never recommend that a person volunteer to care for an Alzheimer's patient. Unless God places such a call, it is almost an impossible task. When God does place such a call, and helps to set up the needed support system, an awesome experience awaits. It is like walking three feet out past the edge of a cliff with God holding your hand.

There were many challenges awaiting me, and no one warned me what the road ahead held. My grandmother's life seemed like the motions of the sea. Just as the waves would come in and go out, she would have good days and bad days, but the tide was receding. Her good days weren't quite as good as they had been, and her bad days were worse. My course of action during this phase of her life was to allow her as much independence as possible and help her with what she couldn't handle anymore.

She lived with me in my home during the remainder of her life. I built her a special room with a southern exposure and a large picture window facing a countryside view. Each day light would flood the room with the new morning.

My grandmother was a dearly beloved member of my household. When I first started taking care of her, the only way I could do it was to postulate that I would take care of her until she could no longer take a bath by herself. After all, she was my grandmother. There was some modesty in me, whether false or true I'm not sure, but this is where I drew a line. That day finally came. Some days she could bathe herself, some days she couldn't. I had a terrible inner struggle. *What should I do now, God? Should I take her to a nursing home?* I asked God if He would strengthen me so I could handle something I had never intended to do. After much inner turmoil, I came to the conclusion that I would help her with bathing. It seems insignificant now but it was a giant concern then. So I moved the line. I agreed to bathe her but determined that when she could no longer use the rest room and take care of her personal hygiene, I would turn the matter over to my father, and let him take it from there. I chose to continue on until then. But that day came too. Some days she could deal with her necessities, some days she couldn't. At times she would have an episode of incontinence. There would be a big mess everywhere and I would have to clean it and her up. Once again I was faced with struggle. Should I continue on? *What should I do now, God? I feel like You called me to be here, but I don't want to deal with this mess. I don't want to handle this situation. Why do* I *have to do this? Why is this coming into her and my lives?* I wrestled with God until I finally came to the realization that it was I, not the situation, that was the problem. I was drawing lines in terms of my obedience to God's call in my life. One day I made the decision to accept the responsibility unreservedly and do whatever was required no matter what happened. An incredible peace came over me at that point and it was very, very comforting.

There were many other challenges to both my grandmother and me during the ensuing years, and many things happened because of my commitment to her care.

She provided for me the gift of time to mature in the practice of receiving godly instruction and applying it in faith to my life; time to develop the ability to hear God's voice and direction for my life; time to learn and practice loyalty, service, endurance, and compassion. She brought my divorced dad and mom, my sister, and me together in a concerted family love effort. She changed all who came into our home: my family, my friends, health-care professionals, and at one time even a newspaper reporter who came to do a special report on the elderly, with her and our situation a keynote for the article. She impacted everyone who came to our home through the example of family love and dedication. She, with dignity, gave the ultimate gift of herself every day as she continued to suffer and endure. She gave much more to those of us who responded to her needs than we could give to her.

Shortly before her death, I became intrigued with the ancient design of the holy temple in the Old Testament. I would read about it and in my quiet time before God meditate on it. I pictured going through the ritual of the ancient priests: into the outer court, the inner court, and the holy of holies. Visualizing the mercy seat in meditation I would be still and listen for God's personal direction. To my astonishment there was what appeared to be water flowing out of the mercy seat. This, I thought, also was biblical. I wondered if this was the water of life that Jesus had talked about.

Many years passed since I had begun taking care of my grandmother. She was no longer in the same physical condition she had been in at the beginning. She now had to be turned every hour during the day. She had a feeding tube providing her water and nourishment for life, and a urinary catheter. We took care of her and loved her. During this phase of her life we talked to her as if she totally understood all that was going on around her and everything that was said in her presence even though she was unable to respond. Many times a day I would tell her I loved her. I would hug her. I would also relate to her by touching her and rubbing her arms, holding her hand, and running my fingers through her hair. I would let her know she was always special, that she was always giving me a greater gift than I could possibly give her, and that she was very, very dearly loved. I would also play Bible tapes in her room so that the Word of God could surround her, and together we listened to favorite radio ministers who became our friends and loyal confidants throughout the entire ordeal. After caring for her nonstop for fifteen years she had become much, much more than just a grandmother.

The day of my grandmother's passing finally came. Being the victor in so many wrestling matches with death, she lost just once. I can never forget the night her life came to its end. The silence and emptiness were overwhelming, yet constant. The pattern of waking up every hour to go turn her was not breakable. The lessons of loyalty that had taken so many years to learn now seemed somehow useless. The phrase I had told her so often, "Don't worry, Granny, I'll take care of you," also seemed meaningless.

By the next morning I was emotionally spent. I had slept some on and off but I had been used to that out of necessity for years. The pattern of starting off the day with a quiet time of Bible reading and meditation benefited me greatly on this day. After reading my devotional and Bible I turned to meditation. I began to meditate on the holy temple. I went through the ancient rituals in my mind and through the different courts. In meditation I knelt before the mercy seat and began to visualize the area surrounding the ark of the covenant. To my astonishment, it seemed to me that my grandmother was standing there with her one-day-old son who had died earlier in her life, the uncle I had never known, in one arm, and a cup in the hand of the other. Holding the cup under the flow of the living water coming out of the mercy seat, she filled it. My grandmother then gave some to her baby and drank some herself. She looked at me with the most loving eyes and with the sweetest voice said, "Don't be sad for me one minute, Buddy. It's just like I woke up out of a nightmare."

Something happened to me in that moment. My grief was absolutely gone. I sensed a wholeness and completeness to my life that I had never experienced before.

When I went to the funeral I noticed people looking at me, expecting to see me broken by the ordeal, see me weep. Every one of them had a little bit of a question mark in their eyes, wondering how I was taking this so well and why it was so easy for me. Instead, I was happy that day. I was smiling and I even laughed a little too loud at one joke a cousin told me. There was no sadness. That moment at the fount of living water with my grandmother and her newborn had taken care of it. God had extended even in this most difficult situation His love, His truth, His power, His supernatural time of refreshing, and His ability to give me an understanding of the completeness of the whole process of that period in her life and mine.

I have come to realize that there is a great safety net of God's loving hands that would catch each one of us even in death. I now know for certain that God faithfully and lovingly empowers His special plan for each one of us as we obediently follow His call in our life. He consistently provides guidance every bit of the way while supplying every necessity, every dollar, and every person needed for success. I still miss my grandmother. I most likely always will miss her until I am with her again. Even though she has gone ahead into the heavenly realm I now realize that all of God's children are just one breath—our last breath—away from where she is.

Alfred F. Eckhardt

Alfred F. Eckhardt writes today from Helotes, Texas.

THE GUEST OF HONOR

Mabel McKee

Grandfather was Ruth's all in all—even though he was not her grandfather by birth. She often wondered where she really came from. The only clue she had was a rather crude locket.

Perhaps someday . . .

Every day brought its own collection of invitations to Valentine parties to the Merrill home. Grandfather, who always sorted the mail at the table, boasted, "This Merrill family is the most popular in town. Everybody, even the baby, has been invited to at least one party except Ruthie and me. The town leaves us alone then, knowing we always have our own Valentine Day celebration."

The slender girl with the dusky eyes and dark curly hair, who sat opposite him, flashed Grandfather a smile. Back of that smile, however, her beautiful lips twitched a minute. Everybody quite missed the pain in that twist. "Regular party with no variations, Grandfather," she said, smiling.

Her fingers slipped down into the pocket of her rose sport dress. Two dainty little invitations were pressed more tightly than before into that pocket, invitations to parties that loomed as great adventures. It had taken coaxing to get old Martha to slip these out of the mail when the postman handed it to her. Old Martha, however, unlike the other servants in the Merrill home, knew the story of Ruth's coming to the Merrill home.

She could not know, though, that often Ruth longed for more young friends and more gay times like the real Merrill girls had. She didn't know, either, that sometimes Ruth, safe in the privacy of her own room, shed a few tears for this youth she was missing. She would then dream of herself in a party frock like those Elizabeth and Myra often wore of evenings.

She rarely left Grandfather, however, who at eighty-nine found himself one of the few members of the "old guard" still living. Without Ruth his evenings were lonely.

Ruth had come to the Merrill home on Valentine's Day. Grandfather Merrill, veteran of the Civil War and head of the Merrill Wholesale Company, had brought her. That had been fifteen years before. Close to midnight he had come back from a reunion of his company at the organization's home for orphan children whose fathers or grandfathers had fought in the war.

His cab had clattered up to the Merrill home and awakened Martha, who was then middle-aged and who had been with Grandmother Merrill for close to twenty years before the latter had died. Donning a bathrobe, Martha had run downstairs to open the door for Grandfather.

The first thing she saw when he stepped on the porch was the great bundle in his arms. It made even the soldierly old man stoop a little. Before she could voice her wonder, Grandfather had chuckled. "Yes, it's a baby, Martha, a little girl from the orphanage. She hung on to my hand all day and screamed to come home with me. I couldn't leave a crying child. The matron told me to just bring her home for a few days, and when she got homesick for the other children, I could bring her back."

"The matron told you!"

"Now, Martha." Grandfather looked sheepish. "To be exact, she finally agreed with my proposition that I do that."

Martha was now unwrapping the great Scotch shawl Grandfather had bundled around the child. She looked in delight at the little girl, close to three years old, whose dusky curls were tangled, whose thick lashes fairly lay on her cheeks, and whose mouth was the most beautiful baby mouth Martha had ever seen. She patted the thin little body so different from the chubby little blond girls of the Merrill home. "She's beautiful, Colonel Merrill," smiled Martha, "but powerful skinny."

Mrs. John Merrill, Grandfather's favorite daughter-in-law, whose boast was that she was the only wife of a Merrill boy asked to live in Grandfather's great mansion of a home, welcomed the little visitor the next morning. "We're going to keep her long enough to get her hearty and strong," she said.

Ruth, however, who called herself "Rujah" and jabbered constantly about horses, cows, and bunny, had never gone back to the orphanage. A terrible fire had destroyed the great building and all its records a few days later. The matron, a few other employees, and several tiny tots perished in the flames.

Grandfather Merrill had hugged the dark-haired little girl tightly in his arms as they read of the tragedy. After that no one ever mentioned Ruth's leaving the old man who loved her so much.

John Merrill had tried to find out something about the dusky little visitor, but failed completely. The only thing anyone knew for certain was that the girl was an orphan, completely alone in the world.

When Ruth was ten years old, Grandfather Merrill had told her the story of her coming. He did not want strangers to tell her that.

Her position in the Merrill home had become a strange one as far as the girls were concerned. When they were alone, she was like a sister. When their friends came, however, she was just "Grandfather's little girl," to stay with him in his room like a nurse.

Myra and Elizabeth were in college now, but they came home over weekends, for their school was just twenty miles away. They came home for parties, too, and their gay talk was always about their girl friends and their masculine admirers. No one in the Merrill home seemed to realize that Ruth longed to share their good times.

That is, no one except Norman, the sixteen-year-old son of the Merrill home. It was to Ruth he took his geometry and

English for aid, remembering that in high school she had been an honor roll student.

To her he stormed, "I think you're crazy, Rujah, to let the girls high hat you the way they do except when they want to borrow your things. What will you do when Grandfather has to go west?"

The quick tears sprang to her eyes when Norman asked that. She felt as though he were a real brother then. That was the reason she showed him the cheap little heart locket with the imitation opal in it one day and told him the story about it. Grandfather had given it to her the day he told her of her coming to the Merrill home. "It was around my neck," she explained. "It's worthless. I know Grandfather thinks I've thrown it away. But I've a feeling that it will someday help me find out what my name really is."

Boyishly Norman had stiffened. "Merrill is your name," he declared.

Alone Ruth thought the matter out. Merrill was indeed a good name. She was proud to carry it. If she should find out, however, that she was as well born as Myra and Elizabeth, then they would love her more. They would ask her to join the Modern Arts Club and the Arcadians. Of all the clubs to which Myra and Elizabeth belonged, Ruth hungered only for these two. The Arcadians did great charity work as well as had beautiful parties. The Modern Arts Club was for girls who dreamed of being writers, artists, sculptors, or something like that. Hidden in Ruth's desk were dozens of little poems and stories she had written.

After Norman was gone, Ruth dangled the cheap little locket from her fingers. "In stories," she laughed hungrily, "this would have been hung on my neck by my mother. Through it I would find some wealthy relatives or some who had done something famous. But in real life, never. Besides, no mother would hang such a heavy thing around a baby's neck."

She did not throw it away, however. Instead, it was dropped into the drawer with her trinkets and forgotten for a while. That very afternoon Mrs. Rufus Stout, president of the Daughters of Veterans, stopped to tell Grandfather Merrill about the annual Lincoln's birthday party the Daughters were giving for the few remaining members of his post. "You'll like it, Colonel," she said. "We're having two speakers, both very good. One is Colonel Masterson from Philadelphia. You've heard of him, I'm sure."

"Heard of him!" Grandfather snorted his interruption. "He and I fought together at Chickamauga." He started reminiscing.

Before he was through, Mrs. Stout looked weary. Myra, who happened to be in the room, slipped out; Elizabeth openly read a magazine. Only John Merrill, who adored his father, and Ruth sat alert, drinking in every word.

"Ruthie will come with me," Grandfather Merrill said. "I would like for her to be the flag bearer."

Mrs. Stout smiled at the dusky, slender girl. "Wonderful!" she declared. "And then there's to be another speaker, a young attorney from the capitol. My husband says he is a coming statesman.

"He likes the girls, John says, and I've promised to introduce him to some pretty ones while he's here. I'll start with Ruth."

Grandfather Merrill's face beamed. After Mrs. Stout had gone, he turned toward his daughter-in-law. "I'm going to write a check and I want you and Ruthie to have a shopping spree. Buy her something frilly for that evening."

Mrs. Merrill laughed girlishly. Shopping was always a delight to her. "Make it a big check," she stipulated. "I'm going to get her something gorgeous, though I'm not expecting much from

Mrs. Stout's young man. You know what freakish people she does pick up."

I wish it were a valentine party, thought Ruth wistfully. *I haven't been to a valentine party for ages and ages.*

The new pink taffeta evening frock, dainty pumps, and old-fashioned lace mitts that were bought on the shopping expedition were a sensation at the Merrill home when Ruth donned them for the Lincoln's birthday party. While the rest of the members of the Merrill family praised the new outfit, Mrs. Merrill, with motherly solicitude, was afraid the dress was a trifle too long, and pushed a stubborn curl into position. She looked at Ruth's shoulder bouquet which Grandfather had ordered for her. "Those roses just match the little mesh bag I gave you at Christmas," she declared. "And it's just the thing to carry tonight."

That was how Ruth happened to see the cheap little heart-shaped locket with its imitation opal that night. It was in the drawer with the bag. Being in a mood which expects wonders to happen, she took out the locket and fastened it around her neck.

When Grandfather Merrill and Ruth reached Memorial Hall, the program had just started. As soon as they were seated, right at the front of the room, Ruth saw the speakers of the evening: old Colonel Masterson from Philadelphia and a stalwart young fellow from the state capitol. He was not a freak at all, but very boyish and human.

Ruth continued to stare at him. His face seemed to come from the pages of some book she had read long ago. Quietly he talked about the boy Lincoln, his old homestead in Indiana, and the state's plan to pay honor to its greatest citizen by making the homestead into a state park.

"It's a dream of my youth, this park," he ended. "I want this young Lincoln honored. He appeals to me because my grandfather was a soldier in his war and because I was once a motherless boy, too, trying to help my father eke a living out of those barren clay hills. Father died and I was taken to the orphanage your organization helps support. So you can see I owe everything to the men of '61."

Ruth knew instantly he meant the orphanage from which Grandfather Merrill had taken her fifteen years before. She lifted her program. There was his name, Benjamin Morris. *Benny Morris—Benny—Bunny,* she whispered slowly to herself. *Bunny, Bunny!*

A little laugh escaped her, a little girl laugh, gay and happy and expectant. She must see this young man to find out if he remembered her. She saw to it that Grandfather was comfortably seated and talking to his old friend, Colonel Masterson, before she slipped away to lay a timid hand on the arm of the young orator. "Did any little girl ever call you Bunny when you were at the orphanage?" she asked.

Two firm hands went onto Ruth's shoulders while the young man stared into her face. A hand tipped up her chin and then twisted it slightly to one side. "Dusky eyes, a stubborn curl, and the dimple caused when you bumped into a rusty nail at the orphanage barn. Yes, you really are little Ruth McPheters!

"But," he shook his head. "How can you be here? They said you burned in the fire." As if fascinated, then, he touched the locket on the chain around Ruth's neck. "That's the bauble I bought for you at the state fair, when Silas took me to Indianapolis," he laughed.

Ruth remembered Grandfather then. After being sure he was still comfortable, she let Benjamin Morris lead her to a secluded spot where she told him the story of her coming to the Merrill home. She ended with the wonder always in her heart about her name, her own people.

"Nobody can tell you better than I, Rujah," laughed the young man. "Your father and mine died in the same typhoid fever epidemic. Your mother brought you to the orphanage to which they had taken me, just a few months before she died. I promised to always look out for you. Then came the fire. I was out at the orphanage farm the night it happened. The superintendent perished, and they said you—were dead too.

"Your grandfather and mine fought with Colonel Masterson at Antietam," he went on. "They—"

Ruth laughed gaily. Oh, she was worthy of Grandfather Merrill now. She was the granddaughter of a fellow soldier. Excitedly she jumped up and ran over to Grandfather to hug him before everybody.

"My dear," Grandfather's hand slipped into hers anxiously, "would you mind very much if I deserted you this Valentine Day? You see Colonel Masterson is staying over. Mrs. Stout wants to give a dinner for him that evening and—"

Benjamin Morris had reached into his pocket while the old man was talking and taken out an envelope. When Grandfather paused, he began, "A friend sent me this invitation to a Valentine dinner party when he found out I was coming here. Bill Lawton is his name. We were good friends at college. His sister's club is giving the party. They want me to be a guest of honor."

Ruth clasped her hands tightly together. The invitation was from the Arcadians.

Young Morris was continuing. "There are two tickets here, Colonel, and if you don't mind, I'll take your granddaughter to this party to make sure I manage the knives and forks right."

The little dimple made by the rusty nail quivered delightfully.

Ruth's laugh was charged with happiness. Her forehead even went a delicate pink when Benjamin whispered, "You might as well get used to going to parties with me, Rujah dear, for I'm going to spend a lot of time in this town from now on."

Mabel McKee

Mabel McKee, early in the twentieth century, was responsible for some of the most memorable inspirational literature in print.

THE ELK TOOTH DRESS

Dorothy Johnson

Natalie didn't want to go to the big show. And if she did, she certainly didn't want to go wearing Indian clothes. But Grandma had a way of getting her way. And not just with Grandpa. So Natalie went, in Grandma's elk tooth dress.

And then Natalie took one look at George Standing in the Water.

Joe Red Crane came over to talk about our going to the Indian Institute in Missoula. It is a big gathering at the University with meetings for several days, to talk about the problems of Indians, and have we got problems! Grandpa said that this year he would let the professors talk about the problems and he would just as soon be in the big show in the University Field House after they got the problems all talked about.

Sometime, maybe, I will learn how to get around Grandma, but Grandpa still can't do it, and he has been married to her for thirty-five years. I am only sixteen years old. They are both old-fashioned, but Grandpa is not so stubborn.

Grandpa wanted to wear his own grandfather's feather war bonnet in the big show, but Joe Red Crane talked him out of it. That shows the difference between Grandpa and Grandma. Nobody ever talked her out of anything.

"This old war bonnet is the real thing," Grandpa argued in the Salish language. "The feathers are broken because it is old and been kicked around."

"It don't look like much," Mr. Red Crane said. "Now we want to look real good, don't we? You know how those Blackfeet dress up all fancy. They are stylish dancers, too. You want us Flatheads to put on a good show, don't you?"

Grandpa snorted and said in English, "Good show? Our folks used to lick the daylights out of them Blackfeet when we went hunting buffalo on the east side of the mountains. Blackfeet! Humph!"

"But you weren't there," Mr. Red Crane said.

Grandpa yelped, "Hey, what tribe you belong to, Joe? You Blackfeet now, Joe?"

"Now, now," said Mr. Red Crane. "I'm Flathead, like you."

"You are no Flathead," said Grandpa. "You are some kind of

mail-order Indian. Where did you get that feather outfit you wore at the Arlee Powwow? Sent away for it someplace, that's what you did. And what about them tail feathers you got? Our people didn't wear tail feathers in the old days. I wouldn't be caught dead in tail feathers."

He switched back to Salish again. "I am not going to dance in Missoula," he said, and started to put the broken old war bonnet back in its box.

Mr. Red Crane got worried, but he knows how to get around Grandpa, who is old-fashioned.

"We better smoke about this," he said.

So Grandpa got out his old, long pipe and they sat on the floor in the parlor. Grandma didn't even say anything about ashes on her nice clean floor, because she likes old-fashioned ways.

After a while, Mr. Red Crane said, "You are the best dancer on the Flathead Reservation."

"There is no doubt about that," answered Grandpa.

"You got real style," Mr. Red Crane said.

"I sure have," said Grandpa.

"You don't even have to wear bells on your ankles when you dance. You don't have to dress up or anything. You get a tremendous hand just because you dance so good."

"That is absolutely right," said Grandpa.

"So you will dance at the Indian Institute in Missoula, maybe?"

"Now you put it that way, maybe I will," said Grandpa. "But I won't wear tail feathers or no mail-order war bonnet. I will just wear my beaded vest."

"You will also wear pants," Grandma said to him over her shoulder.

Grandpa said, "All the time I meant to wear pants. Women should stay out of serious conversations."

"There would be serious conversations if you went to Missoula with no pants," Grandma answered.

Then Mr. Red Crane got around to noticing me. I was doing my homework, and you can bet it is hard to memorize irregular French verbs when you are listening to a conversation that switches from English to Salish and back.

"We got to have a nice display of art work for the exhibit," he said. "You going to bring something pretty, Natalie? I bet you are. Some nice beadwork?"

"I don't like beadwork," I said. "It's old-fashioned. I don't think I will go anyway. Not unless I can get my hair cut short and have a permanent."

Grandma said to the wall, "Natalie will go, and she will not have a permanent. She will wear her hair in braids like she was meant to. She has not got her exhibit finished yet, but she will. It is a bag all covered with beads." Grandma switched to Salish and muttered, "She is lazy. Bad girl."

I am only kind of lazy and not very bad, but I did not argue, because getting a permanent is something we have not agreed about for two years or more.

Joe Red Crane saved his talk with Grandma till last, because it was going to be the toughest.

"And you will wear your fringed buckskin dress with the elk teeth all over it," he said to her with a big smile, "and you will be in the Grass Dance."

"I will not do any such thing," said Grandma. "I am going to wear my go-to-town clothes and sit in the audience and watch everybody and see whether my old man is wearing his pants. Natalie can wear my dress with the elk teeth if she wants to. I guess she won't want to, though, because she has all these modern ideas."

I almost jumped out of my chair. She had never let me wear that dress before. It is very old and valuable. If I had asked her for it, she would have said, "No, you are careless, you would lose some of the elk teeth."

"That's all settled then," Mr. Red Crane said, getting up off the floor.

After he left, I went to work on Grandma, figuring that if I said no, she would say yes.

"I don't want to get my braids cut off and have a permanent," I said. "I have decided to wear my hair long even if you do have to work so hard brushing it."

"Good thing," she said, "because that is how it is going to be."

At school all the kids were talking about going to Missoula, and when I found out some more about the plans, I got pouty.

"I'm not going to go," I told Grandma. "Mary MacTavish is going to be introduced as a princess because her great-grandfather was a chief and signed some old treaty. She would have flunked algebra if I hadn't helped her with homework. So now she is a princess. Mary MacTavish—some Indian!"

Grandma got a wicked look on her face and said, "The Scottish fur traders were very busy around here in the old days, but not in my family or your grandfather's. Just be proud you're a full-blood and never mind that princess stuff. But you will go."

Now I am glad I went, because it was a lovely time. It was the most wonderful time I can remember.

That was a big affair, that Indian Institute at the University Field House in Missoula. Grandpa even washed the station wagon. He spent so much time on it that Grandma got nervous and said she would rather ride in a car with mud on it than get there after everybody else left. But we got there early.

We had the biggest bunch of people from our reservation because we only had to go a few miles. There were people from tribes all over Montana, strangers, handsome people in beautiful costumes. Second to us, the Blackfeet had the biggest bunch, and Grandma said, "Huh! The women wear rouge."

There were more languages being spoken than I had ever heard before—Indian languages, all different. Absolutely nobody said one word in French. Sometimes I wonder why I go to all the trouble with those irregular verbs. One good thing about Salish, nobody fusses about grammar. You just talk it.

It was a wonderful time, the gathering of all those dark, dignified people—my people, even if they were from other tribes with other languages. The whites came too, of course, lots of them, but they were just there to see us.

In the big crowd, we lost track of Grandpa.

"Now where is that Indian exhibit?" Grandma muttered, and I said, "I don't want to go see that."

"I should think you wouldn't," she answered, "but we are going to see it anyway."

It was embarrassing because I never did finish my beadwork exhibit and Grandma had to. She fussed because she had to do it kind of sloppy so nobody would know it wasn't all mine. But after all, when a girl is a junior in high school and studying French, and she's in a lot of activities, how much time has she got for beadwork?

We found the exhibit. Grandma asked an Indian where it was. She wouldn't ask a white person because she wouldn't admit they might know something she didn't.

Mary MacTavish was hanging around the exhibit, because her

entry for art work was a drawing of Marilyn Monroe that she copied out of a movie magazine. Mary MacTavish, that princess, stood around in her mail-order buckskin dress batting her eyelashes, and I must admit she had two fellows from our football team and two others hanging around with her.

"Oh, hello, Natalie," she said very sweetly, for fear I wouldn't notice all those fellows, and I said, "Hi ya, princess, old kid."

Grandma said in a carrying voice, "We will not look at any drawings copied out of magazines. We will look at the real Indian art. Well, that bag you beaded looks pretty good, Natalie. They displayed it nice."

I kind of nudged my arm against her arm to tell her I was grateful that she didn't give away my guilty secret about not finishing it myself, and she nudged back. When Grandma is for you, she is for you all the way, especially if somebody else is against you.

"Where did that old man of mine go?" she grumbled.

"He just came in," I said, "with a white woman," and Grandma said, "What!"

Grandpa was being very Noble Red Man. He is not very tall, but he can look awful noble. He was just looking past this white woman in a baggy tweed suit and not answering her, and she was getting more and more earnest, pointing at her camera and talking her idea of Indian English: "Me take picture, okay? You stand still, me take nice picture?"

I was so grateful to Grandma for being on my side that I walked over and rescued him for her, because she wouldn't lower herself by chasing after him.

I said to him in Salish, "Come on with me if you want to get away."

The white woman said, "Little girl, maybe you talk English—just tell him I want to take his picture."

So if she wanted to, why didn't she go ahead?

I murmured, *"Je ne parle pas l'anglais. Mon granpère ne parle pas l'anglais."*

She shook her head and said, "Oh, dear. They all talk Indian," and walked away.

Then we three went to the field house and got settled in the front row of the audience.

We looked around and I saw the most beautiful thing I ever laid eyes on. He was tall and lean, in tight jeans and cowboy boots, and he had long hair. Long, thick, glossy braids, even if he was young like me—long hair like the old men, but ah, how pretty it looks on a young fellow!

He was as handsome as a calendar, with a sharp profile and his head held high. He wore a cowboy hat, sort of tipped back so it wouldn't hide the soft way his hair came down over his ears, because he was proud of his hair, and that was right.

Alongside him, all the boys I know look just plain stupid. My heart hurt. I kind of wanted to cry.

I said in a whisper, "Grandma, look."

"Look at what?" she asked. "All those strange Indians?"

Then I saw he was not by himself but in a group of five or six men, all older, but do you know, I hadn't noticed them before. They were Indians but wearing business suits, and a couple of them had braids.

Grandma saw the young man then and said, "Ah." She said something to Grandpa and he looked and said, "Ah."

Then he got up and ambled over to these men halfway across the arena and they all got acquainted and shook hands. The young long-hair didn't talk; he just stood there listening, the way a young man should in the presence of his betters, only generally they don't.

Grandma said, "They are Cheyennes," and I asked, "How can you tell from here?"

"Your grandpa just told me in sign talk," she answered. "If you'd keep your eyes open, you might learn something. The young fellow is going to be in the show." She squinted and added, "His name is something like water."

It just goes to show you how much good French does a girl when something really important comes up. I don't pay much attention to sign talk, it's old-fashioned. We used to use it in grade school when we wanted to make remarks about a new teacher.

"Oh, look at that mail-order princess," I said, shocked. "She is going right over to interrupt the men. She is going to get that Cheyenne boy for herself."

"I don't think she is," said Grandma. "Keep still and trust your grandpa. Sometimes he is a no-good, but in a pinch you can depend on him."

Mary was heading for the men, with two other girls, all giggling and wiggling. But Grandpa fixed her wagon. It was cute how he did it. He never glanced around, never saw those fresh girls right behind him, trying to attract his attention, trying to interrupt. He never saw them, but every time Mary moved a little to one side, he moved too, so his back was always toward her while he talked to the other men.

There was quite a crowd of Indians around there, making a quiet fuss over the long-hair boy. The old people approved because he was conservative, old-fashioned, and the boys hung around because he was twirling a rope, sort of playing with it, and the girls edged up because he was so cute. And I had to stay by Grandma because we are conservative.

Grandma said, "Never mind that phony Minnehaha, making eyes. You make eyes at the ground. . . . Listen, I saw some other women from other reservations with elk teeth on their dresses, but not so many as on the dress you're wearing. Don't you worry."

She dug in the big bag she carried and brought out something. It was her little old short cape embroidered with porcupine quills, dyed in soft colors long ago. She hung it over my shoulders, and I felt warm and cared for because I knew she thought a lot of me and was on my side.

Even when I was a child, not many women were embroidering with porcupine quills; they used all beads because it was easier. This cape was very old, made by my grandmother. The buckskin was soft and gray, not dirty but not glaring white. Wearing it, I felt like a queen and was not very jealous of Princess MacTavish.

The men and boys from our reservation were buckling on the bells they wear on their legs for dancing, and you couldn't hear yourself think. They are big round bells with something noisy inside. And Grandpa had gone over to the middle and started beating a drum. The only thing he doesn't like about a show is that he can't beat a drum and dance at the same time.

Then a man said, "Woof, woof, testing," into the public-address system, and asked everybody to take his seat because the show was going to begin. The young long-hair walked past us with his friends but he did not look our way at all.

Grandma said, "Natalie, stop looking at him all the time."

"What does he wear long hair for if he doesn't want to be looked at?" I answered.

"I don't know what he wants," said Grandma, "but I want you to stop looking. He will think you are bold."

"He doesn't know I'm alive," I moaned, and she said with a satisfied chuckle, "Oh, yes, he does. What do you think your grandpa went over there for? To talk about the hay crop, maybe?"

I was so happy I even stopped staring.

Grandma said, "Doesn't Mary MacTavish look silly with her short hair in that Indian dress from mail order? But you look just right."

"I am a bad girl and lazy," I said. "You had to finish my beadwork."

"Oh, not so bad," she answered, always arguing.

Somebody on the public-address system made a long speech about the significance of all this and named all the tribes that were represented, and then he said the Flatheads would please take their places. So I left Grandma and went drifting out to the arena with the rest of our people and stood with the other girls in the back.

The men sat down in chairs in a long row. The chairs were turned backward because if a man wears tail feathers he has to straddle when he sits down. But Grandpa turned his chair around and leaned back and was comfortable, because he wouldn't be caught dead in those mail-order tail feathers. He had a big silver ornament on each braid, but he wasn't dressed up except for a beaded vest. He wore his pants all right, blue jeans. He wore his silver-rimmed glasses, too, and Grandma didn't like that; she says it is too modern. But he says, "I am nearsighted and I wear glasses. You want me to fall over something and break my neck, maybe?"

Mary MacTavish said to me, "Hi, kid. It's too bad they won't let me present you to the audience. Alice and Elizabeth are my maids-in-waiting, you know. I am going to present them to the audience. But I can't do a thing for you, because their ancestors signed the same treaty mine did, but your ancestors wouldn't sign."

"My ancestors never gave the country away," I said. "They wanted to hang on to it."

"What are you looking at the ground for?" she asked. "Lost something?"

"Indian girls are supposed to be modest," I said. "Didn't anybody ever tell you? I am a full-blood, so I am going to be modest while I've got this elk tooth dress on and this old and valuable embroidered cape all covered with dyed porcupine quills."

"I guess you're just jealous because I'm not going to present you too," Mary MacTavish said.

"I guess you'd better be kind of polite," I said, "if you don't want to flunk French."

Then we had to quit talking, because Mr. Red Crane started to talk on the public-address system, introducing our people.

There were a couple of dances for the men, good and noisy, with all the drumming and all those bells on their legs clanging with every step, and I was in the Grass Dance with Mary and the rest of them.

Mr. Red Crane introduced Princess Mary MacTavish, and she walked forward with her beaded moccasins on her feet and her permanent on her head, looking so modest it would kill you, making eyes at the ground.

"Princess Mary will now present her maids-in-waiting," Mr. Red Crane said, and everybody waited, but she didn't. She was being so modest, she just stood there. So Alice had to walk out by herself, and so did Elizabeth.

Then *they* just stood there, the modest Indian maidens, until the announcer told them twice they could go sit down now.

Then he said, "One of the girls from the Flathead Reservation is wearing a very rare costume, very old, that I am sure you will want to see. Natalie Root Digger, will you please walk forward so the audience can see you?"

Well, I just about died. I went forward about three steps and stood there with my eyes down, feeling those thousands of people staring. He told about the old dress with the elk teeth on it and the precious cape embroidered with porcupine quills, and the people clapped. I went back without anybody telling me.

I never took my eyes off the ground, but I saw that long-hair Cheyenne in the front row sitting by Grandma. She looked good. She wore her black dress with red figures in it, and her best purple silk handkerchief draped around her head in folds, with her long, dark braids looped to hang down under it.

Our people did more dances, and Grandpa would sneak out in front of the rest and kind of clown with his dancing. Every time he did that, the audience would laugh and clap. Then we went out of the arena and finally I got over to where Grandma was. She said in Salish, "Sit down. Lots of room," and the long-hair started to get up out of the way. But Grandma said in English, "Stay there. She's little, she won't crowd you."

He said, "She sure won't," and we sat close because we had to, both looking at the ground but seeing each other just the same.

He had the most wonderful voice, deep and soft and bashful.

The announcer said now the Blackfeet would come in and perform, and Grandma said, "Huh!"

All the other Indians, when they had gone into the arena, had just sort of drifted in. But those Blackfeet came marching to a drum, very slowly, and their leader gave them signals with an eagle wing fan. Real fancy.

The long-hair boy said, "Tourist stuff," and Grandma looked at him with approval.

They did some dances and they were so popular with the silly crowd of white people that they kept right on doing dances. The Cheyenne boy made a thoughtful sound and got up and walked across the arena toward Grandpa and the rest of our Flathead men. In a minute, Grandpa and the others from our reservation started walking from one end of the arena toward the other.

You should have heard it. They didn't do anything but just walk and mind their own business, but when two dozen Indians walk from one place to another with strings of big bells on their legs, not keeping step—well. The racket was so loud, with the clanging of the bells drowning out the Blackfeet drums, that the audience forgot about the Blackfeet dancing, so smart and sassy. People got kind of fidgety and started looking at their programs, and when they clapped for the Blackfeet, Grandma and I clapped for the Flatheads.

Grandma said, "Well, I guess we won *that* battle."

When the young long-hair came back, drifting, Grandma moved over so he would sit between us.

"What's your name, Cheyenne?" she asked.

"George Standing in the Water," he answered.

"You're a smart boy," Grandma said, "and I would like to meet your folks sometime."

He didn't say anything, but he blushed. A blush under a bronze skin is pretty.

"Your folks are old-fashioned?" Grandma asked him, and he knew it was a compliment, and nodded.

"My brother fasted in the Sun Dance last year," he said. "Maybe I will someday."

We don't do the Sun Dance—we have our own customs—but I knew a little about that, and I shivered. The few men who dare to dance the Sun Dance starve and don't drink any water for four days; then they dance until they faint sometimes.

"Maybe we'll come to your reservation sometime," Grandma purred.

"I wouldn't want to see the Sun Dance if anybody I knew was in it," I said, feeling terrible.

"My brother's girl, she was kind of proud of him," George said. So then I thought I could watch him if the time came, and I would be proud too.

The announcer said on the public-address system, "A young Cheyenne from the Tongue River Reservation will demonstrate his skill in roping. I present George Standing in the Water, of the northern Cheyennes."

George went out in the arena, not very far, not looking up at the audience, but as if he were there all by himself with nobody around. It was all quiet, no drumming. He twirled his rope in little circles and big circles. He danced into the spinning rope circle and danced out of it again. The rope was like a live thing that did just what he wanted it to do, and his hands hardly moved, but the rope spun its circle and rippled and flashed like water.

People were taking pictures—flash, flash went the cameras, taking pictures of the fine long-hair. Grandpa's white-woman friend was jumping around in her baggy tweed suit, putting new flash bulbs in her camera and taking pictures and talking to herself.

It was as if George were there all alone, in the big field house, dreaming with the spinning rope. When he stopped, there was nothing dramatic about the stopping. He didn't bow to the audience like some performers do. Why should he bow? He didn't owe them anything. He just gathered up his rope when he was through, while the audience clapped and hollered, and he walked over to sit by us again.

I thought, *I wish I had a camera. I wish I could have a picture of George Standing in the Water to keep forever.*

Somebody made another long speech about the significance of all this, and some other tribes danced, and then the whole show was over. Grandpa drifted over to us, and that white woman in the tweed suit made a dive at him.

"Well, I'll take care of *this,*" said Grandma and marched toward them like an army with banners.

"You going home tonight?" George asked, looking at the ground.

I said, "Yes. To Arlee." *And maybe I will never see you again,* I thought. *That will be worse than if I never had known you were alive.* "Where are you going?"

"Staying at a motel with my friends. Long drive to Tongue River. We'll start early in the morning. Listen, where would a fellow write you a letter if he wanted to, maybe? Just Arlee?"

"That's right. Natalie Root Digger, Arlee, Montana." Then I got really bold. "You know, we dig bitterroot around Missoula in the spring, pretty soon. We're old-fashioned. We don't mind if our friends come dig bitterroot with us. Or maybe you have to go to school."

"This year I have to go to school. I am on the track team. Maybe next year. If your folks come to our rodeo. I ride bucking horses."

"Maybe Grandma and Grandpa would like to go to your rodeo," I answered. "I guess they would probably take me along."

We never looked at each other all that time, but I saw his

black, soft, shining braids, and he saw my braids, and the buckskin dress trimmed with elk teeth and the little cape with the faded-color porcupine quill embroidery.

"Well, so long," he said.

I said, "Okay. See you around."

He walked away, so lithe and slim, and my heart wanted to cry.

My folks came back, with their faces straight, but I could tell they were laughing inside about something. I didn't feel like laughing.

"Well, that white woman got your grandpa's picture," Grandma said. "It's hard talking this Injun English she likes, but I got the idea across that she could take his picture if she would send me a print; also she has to send me some other pictures that are on the same roll of film."

"That's nice," I said with my heart jumping. Because she had taken pictures of George while he was spinning the rope.

"Where'd that Cheyenne go?" Grandma asked.

"He had to catch up with his friends. Grandma, he asked us to do their rodeo and I asked him to help us dig bitterroot, and is it all right? If you say it's wrong and I'm not a nice modest girl, I'll just die!"

"It is all right and you are a good girl," she answered. "I think we will maybe go to the Cheyennes' rodeo when the time comes."

When my letter comes from the Tongue River Reservation, it will have his return address on it, I guess. But I wouldn't ask him for it, because it is a good thing to be old-fashioned, even for a girl who is a junior in high school and learning French.

Dorothy Johnson

Dorothy Johnson was one of the leading novelists and short story writers in America during the second half of the twentieth century.

THE MAGICIAN

John M. Hebert

They decided he had grieved long enough. It was time for him to face life again. He disagreed. It took his granddaughter to decide the day.

Barney Johnson had a worried look as he glanced toward the partially opened white doors.

"Karen," he said to the young woman standing beside him, "if this is a disaster, you're not getting me involved in another of your charitable projects." He gave a baleful glare. "Your mother is too busy to help."

"Don't worry, Grandpa," the dark-haired girl spoke cheerfully. "We'll do fine."

She touched the lapels of her sequined costume and looked at Barney's costume—brown trousers, blue denim shirt, and bright red scarf. "We'll knock 'em into the aisles . . . figuratively of course."

Barney smiled, his gray eyes lighting up with pleasant memories. "With your persuasiveness, you've got to be lethal in a courtroom."

She grinned. "I've had my success." *Indeed,* Barney thought, *the greatest may have been along with your mother three weeks ago.*

"Are you nuts?" he had growled at them that day, looking up from his stamp collection. "I haven't performed . . . since your mother . . ." His voice trailed off.

"That's what I mean, Dad," his daughter, Marcie, answered, waving broadly at the cluttered den. "Just look at this place! You've burrowed into this room and tried to let your memories take the place of really living."

"I'm satisfied enough." He picked up the magnifying glass and peered at a stamp.

"Satisfied, pooh," Karen broke in. "I remember, Grandpa, when you said that being satisfied isn't enough. You're really the one who first encouraged me to go to law school."

"You two are double-teamin' me," Barney accused.

"Maybe," Marcie said. "Just think about it, Dad. That's all

we're asking. Some of them are a long way from home, and their families can't visit them much."

"All right, all right! I'll think about it, but do you know what it's like doing a show for a bunch of kids? Like tap dancing in a minefield. Well, I'll think about it." He paused. "Who would be my assistant, smarties?"

"I will, Grandpa," Karen exclaimed gleefully. "Ever since I was three I have wanted to be your assistant. I studied how Grandma did everything." Her eyes shone.

"I'll let you know," Barney said gruffly, looking at the stamp again. Marcie and Karen left after exchanging an *I think we got him* look between themselves.

Barney picked up a picture of his wife. "Well, Bernice, your daughter and granddaughter are conspiring again. Another benefit, like you were always talking me into doing. You taught them well, love."

He placed the picture back on the desk. *Maybe there still is a place for a seventy-year-old magician.* He got up and walked to the three storage cabinets near the fireplace. He'd forgotten the details of some tricks, he found out after a few minutes. He decided that four years without practice was a long time. *And maybe not,* he mused, then turned out the light and went upstairs.

The next morning he called Karen and pretended to be angry. "You! Assistant! Be here at seven sharp. Sharp! And be ready to work. Understand?"

"Yessir, you old grouch, sir, Grandpa sir," Karen answered with delight.

Now Mrs. Washington, the chief nurse, was introducing them. "Children's Memorial Hospital brings you—not Merlin the Magnificent, not Harold the Horrendous, but Barney the Befuddled." They heard weak, scattered applause from the audience.

Barney groaned. "You hear that skimpy applause?"

"Grandpa," Karen said seriously, "remember, some of them can't clap." She took his hand and led him through the double doors.

At first glance, Barney really felt like his stage name; the recreation room was packed with beds, chairs, wheelchairs, and children of all shapes, sizes, and colors. Glancing around, he could see some children were in casts and couldn't clap, and he relaxed slightly.

His granddaughter was speaking. "Good afternoon. I am Karen, the magician's assistant. And this gentleman is not the janitor, but Barney the Befuddled." A few children laughed. Most smiled.

Barney began by telling them that he had found a bunch of magic tricks years ago without instructions, so he didn't actually know how they worked. "Maybe you can help me if I get into trouble?" He looked forlornly and hopefully at his audience.

"Sure!—Yes!—Yes!"

For the next thirty minutes coins, silks, and balls appeared and disappeared mysteriously. His overly dramatic surprise at how some of the tricks turned out brought laughter to faces unused to it.

"I call this one Hippety Hop," he explained as he placed two wooden rabbit silhouettes on the table. "As you can see, one rabbit is white, the other black. Now I'll put these covers on the rabbits." Then he turned each covered rabbit around. "Now—watch!" He took the covers off. "The rabbits have magically changed places!"

"Turn them around, turn them around!" a chorus of young voices chanted.

"Around? You want me to turn them *around?*" Barney asked in mock horror.

"Yes!"

"All right," Barney said reluctantly, "I'll turn them around." He did—and the rabbits were pink and yellow! Screams of surprise and delight filled the room, followed by wild applause.

Two minutes later Barney was shaking hands and handing out small figurines which he produced from under pillows and from behind ears.

Finally he came to a sad-faced girl, a tiny blonde sitting quietly in a wheelchair. "Hello," he said, bending down in front of her. Both of her legs were in stark white casts. "Hello," she answered shyly. "I liked your show."

"Good. I seem to have run out of things from people's ears, though." He pulled a half-dollar out of a brown leather bag while palming a small figurine. "I don't suppose you'd be interested in a souvenir fifty-cent piece instead?" he asked while making the Bobo Switch[7] into his left hand.

"Well . . . ," she began politely.

"If not, how about a . . ." Barney opened his left hand to reveal a miniature silver unicorn.

"A unicorn! Oh, thank you!" she piped, then leaned forward and hugged the smiling magician.

"I thought I'd gotten rid of all the small unicorns," he said a short time later in the hospital coffee shop. "They were your grandmother's favorite animal."

[7] *A magician's trick.*

"You did great, Grandpa," Karen answered softly.

He took his granddaughter's hand. "The real magician today, and three weeks ago, was you. You convinced me to come out of my shell and get involved again. Thank you, dear."

John M. Hebert

John M. Hebert wrote for popular magazines during the second half of the twentieth century.

GRANDMOTHER'S END OF THE ICE CREAM

Annie Hamilton Donnell

Once upon a time about the only ice cream you could get you had to hand-crank. Grandma was bone tired, and then "company" came—Terry, Olive, and little Puss-in-boots—and demanded ice cream.

How could she crank it when she was so exhausted?

Grandmother dropped wearily into a chair. Her sweet face was full of the little tired lines that were nearly always there on Tuesdays. She held up one slender hand with the fingers spread.

"Churning's done—thumb," she said, folding down the thumb; "ironing's done—first finger; beds are made—thimble finger; dishes washed—third finger."

Only the little finger was left, standing up in the wobbly, little-finger way of standing up.

"The little finger stands for dinner," smiled Grandmother. "That *isn't* done! Now, when one has company, I wonder what one gets for dinner—"

There was a stir across the room. The "company" with one accord scrambled to its feet and formed in line.

"Ice cream!" in chorus.

"Oh," said tired Grandmother. Then she said "Oh" again. She had not thought of ice cream! Dear, no, not ice cream! She lowered her spectacles from her pretty white hair to her nose, and glanced up at the clock.

"It's after ten," she said. "It takes a good while sometimes to freeze ice cream. I don't suppose the company would like it unfrozen. There's some nice, soft custard out in the pan—"

The company made a wry face—three wry faces.

"That wouldn't be ice cream, Grandma," pouted Olive.

"Nothing but just *custard!*" pouted Terrence. Terrence was Olive's twin, and always did the things she did. The third "company" was little Puss-in-boots.

"I'd ruvver have I-scream a good dealer," Puss said.

Tired Grandmother got up stiffly, a patient smile on her dear old face, then sat down again with a sudden twinge of rheumatism. Olive was afraid it meant no ice cream for dinner, and

Olive was ice cream hungry. Weren't all three of the company ice cream hungry? Hadn't they talked about having it *sure* when they went to spend the day with Grandma? Grandma always gave folks two saucerfuls—

"We s'posed we'd have it," Olive said in an injured tone.

"Because we're company, that's why. We s'posed you'd give your company—"

"Ice cream," smiled tired Grandmother. "Well, dears, you shall have it, but you will have to wait till supper—it's too late to freeze it for dinner. Will supper do?"

"Oh, yes'm, thank you," Olive said politely, and of course, Terry said, "Oh, yes'm," politely too.

Supper was farther away than dinner, but it would do. And custard was pretty good for dessert. The company was not greedy—just ice cream hungry. Usually it was quite a thoughtful company, and noticed the little tired lines in Grandmother's face, but not today.

Grandmother got dinner and cleared it away. It seemed to her she grew more and more tired. It was fortunate the time for naps was near. Dear, dear, she had forgotten the children's ice cream!

"If Father was only at home to chop the ice!" she sighed gently. Grandfather's being away made it so much harder—he always knew just how much salt to mix with the ice, and he always turned the crank of the big freezer.

"Creak, creak, creak—one, two, three, four—*creak, creak*— five, six, seven." Still the handle went round just the same, and tired Grandmother knew the cream had not yet thickened.

The company was playing at housekeeping out in the grape arbor. It was pleasant and rustly out there, with the leaves everywhere whispering things to each other. Olive said it was beautiful spending the day at grandmother's, wasn't it? And Terry echoed, wasn't it!

"And there's I-scream a-comin'!" chanted Puss-in-boots, clapping and dancing about in great glee.

"Goody!"

"I'm glad we asked for it, aren't you? Grandma might not have remembered our—our ice-cream 'tooth.' "

"Teeth," corrected Olive—"yours and mine and Pussy's. Yes, indeed, I'm glad *we* remembered!"

"I hope there'll be chock-erlate in," Puss said, "and that 'minds me to wish we'd asked for two kinds."

"I wish we had!"

"Maybe we can now—come on, let's hurry like everything!"

The company was in good racing trim. There was a scurry of nimble little feet, and the three little housekeepers arrived, breathless, at the back porch. Olive got there a little in advance.

"Oh, Grandma, can't we have two kinds of ice—" then she stopped. A strange little change came over her round, brown face. For an instant she looked at tired Grandmother in the kitchen rocker, then noiselessly she sped away to meet the rest of the company.

"Oh, sh, sh, *sh!"* she panted softly. "You come with me, but *sh!* Don't do a thing but look at Grandma."

She was fast asleep in the old, stuffed rocking-chair. Her head had fallen back a little, sidewisely, and her dear old face wore a patient look. The weary fingers had released their hold on the crank of the big red freezer.

"Sh!" whispered Olive, but there was no need of it. All the company was sh-ing. They stole away on tiptoes back to the grape arbor.

"She's *very* tired," Olive said severely. "Aren't you 'shamed of yourselves for asking for ice cream?"

"You went and asked the first ask yourself, Olive Tripp! And if you've gone and 'most killed Grandmother—"

"Oh, it was us all! We've all 'most killed her!" wailed Olive in sudden remorse. "And she's the dearest, grandmotherest grandmother! We never thought of *her* end o' the ice cream."

"No, we never," groaned Terrence.

"We just thinked of our end," Pussy lamented.

They lapsed into shamed, gloomy silence. It was awful to sit there in the grape arbor and feel like—like—pigs! And what made it worse, they could distinctly hear a grunting sound in the direction of Grandpa's pigpen.

"They sound like *relations,"* Olive groaned.

When Grandmother woke up, in the late afternoon, the first thing she saw was a jagged piece of white wrapping paper propped up conspicuously on the top of the freezer. It was covered over with great lead-pencil words. She felt in her soft white hair for her glasses and read it—not once, but twice, three times:

> We are Pigs, but Pussy is onley a little one. We nevver thort of your end of the ice scream. We have gorn Home for Fear youl finnish makeing it and it would Choak us. Please don't Wake UP, but keep rite on Resting. We are sorry weve most killed you, Honest.
>
> Terry and Me and Puss

"The little dears!" murmured the rested grandmother.

Annie Hamilton Donnell
(1862–?)

Annie Hamilton Donnell, late in the nineteenth century and early in the twentieth, was one of the most beloved family writers in America. Her favorite subjects were small children. Besides writing prolifically for family magazines, she also wrote books such as *Meeting Cousin Agatha* (1898), *Rebecca Mary* (1905), *The Very Small Person* (1906), and *Miss Theodosia's Heartstrings* (1916).

THE SHABBY LITTLE HOUSE

Irene S. Woodcock

Priscilla hated to admit it, but she was ashamed of their shabby house. Oh, to be able to live in mansions like Angela Seers did! And when the girls visited, Grandpa would be sure to wander in just as though he were invited to.

Sure enough . . .

"It's my turn to entertain the girls this time, Mother, and I feel that I just can't do it."

Mrs. Brown glanced up from her sewing at Priscilla's flushed face; then carefully cut a thread and inserted it in her needle.

"But why, dear?" she asked.

"Oh, Mother! You don't understand. I can't make you. But—but—our house is so different. It's so little and shabby, and has a sort of run-down-at-the-heels look. There isn't another girl in the club that hasn't a beautiful house in which to entertain. Not that I don't love my home, Mother. I do in a way. But still—" She paused a moment and then continued.

"Then there's Grandpa. He just won't go out and leave us alone. If he isn't in the room when the girls get here, he comes in and sits and watches and listens to all we say. It's so embarrassing. It seemed, the last time, that I could never ask anyone here again."

"But they all had a pleasant time?" Mother's sentence was a question.

"They said they did, of course," returned Priscilla. "But that doesn't mean anything. It's just polite to tell your hostess you've had a nice time."

Her mother hesitated. "I think that part could be passed over very nicely," she said at last, slowly. "One could say 'Good-by, Priscilla; it was very kind of you to ask me here and do so much to make it pleasant.' That would be true and not unkind, for the real hostess does exert herself for her guests. I am sorry you feel as you do about the house," she added. "It isn't very elegant, of course; but it seems to be the best that Dad and I can manage at present."

Priscilla's arms were about her mother's neck, and a warm kiss was imprinted on her soft cheek.

"It was thoughtless of me, Mother darling, to speak of it. It's plenty good enough for me, of course. Only sometimes I wish—Angela Seers is in town," she finished abruptly. "She's coming."

Mrs. Brown straightened a little. Angela Seers, then, was the real cause of this outburst. It was unreasonable, of course. She had known Angela's father and mother when they were children. It chanced that John Seers inherited a fortune, and after marriage had gone to the city to live in accordance with his wealth. Every year Angela came to make her aunt a visit. She would have no scruples about inviting the Seers family into her home.

"My dear," she said, and her voice was very gentle. She wished to thoroughly understand and to be understood by this twentieth-century daughter of hers. She wished her to see that the standards of good breeding in her girlhood days were the standard of good breeding still. "I always have felt that if my home had the real home atmosphere, I would not be ashamed to entertain king or potentate within its walls. As for Angela Seers—" her voice shook a little with suppressed feeling—"I am sure that she has no more to boast of than you have."

Priscilla stared at her mother, only half comprehending. Mother just didn't realize that the Seers were so very wealthy—mother had such old-fashioned ideas; that Angela had everything; that she was accustomed to being entertained within the most beautiful homes in the country; that she spent part of practically every summer traveling abroad. Priscilla made no reply, and left for the kitchen to start preparations for supper.

The days passed rapidly, and no further reference was made to the conversation until the day before Priscilla was to entertain the sewing club to which she belonged. Then she entered the kitchen with an armful of dresser covers and some rugs.

"I thought I'd wash these, Mother, for you know the girls are coming tomorrow."

She worked busily all the morning, and restored rugs and covers to their first freshness. But the old shabbiness persisted. There was that spot in the living-room rug which was so worn it seemed as if it must wear through before the next day. Even the most careful mending of the several fine holes that had begun to make their appearance in the curtains could not hide the fact that they were very old. Nothing whatever could be done about the two chairs that sagged so that they were merely hollows. And the dining-room wallpaper was faded beyond pretense of concealment. Priscilla surveyed the result of her work with decided dissatisfaction and a lump in her throat.

It was home, of course, and very dear to her as such. But oh, such a shabby little home! Such a contrast to those of the other club members and that of Angela Seers! When the next day came, bringing sunshine and fresh breezes, Priscilla took heart. It had been a wet, rainy season, and this sunshine was very welcome.

Perhaps I can entertain them mostly on the porch, she thought.

But as the hours slipped by, she knew better. The sunshine was hidden by clouds, a few spatters of rain made their appearance; then followed an abrupt change of wind, making sitting out of doors an impossibility. She lighted a wood fire in the living-room grate, and drew some chairs close to it. That was at least cheerful. She said nothing more to her mother about her feelings. Mother didn't understand; she couldn't, from her old-fashioned viewpoint. There was nothing to do but to make the best of it. And this Priscilla proceeded to do in her usual thorough way. She carried her head high, and her cheeks were flushed as she answered the first ring at the doorbell. This was followed so quickly by others that she had no time to think of anything but the comfort of her guests.

As she had predicted, Grandpa appeared early upon the scene, and settled himself where he could watch them at their work, and an occasional chuckle from his corner reminded them that he was on hand, listening and enjoying the company in his own way. He had dressed carefully for the occasion in his best black suit, a black and lavender striped tie, and a fresh boiled shirt. His thin locks were brushed smooth, and the wrinkled cheeks wore a faint flush. A sudden tenderness filled Priscilla's heart as she eyed him. She felt that he was very old, very dear, very lovable. A quick defiance seized her. The girls shouldn't criticize his being there. He belonged to her: he was part of the shabby little house, and she wanted him just where he was. His faded blue eyes were sparkling. He leaned a trifle forward on his cane. The talk had touched upon the town and some of its old landmarks. It seemed to loosen his tongue, and he entered with zest into the conversation.

Priscilla's cheeks grew a shade rosier. She hoped the girls would understand. They must understand. She was filled with a mixture of love toward her grandfather and anger toward them; she was ready to fight, if need be, for the one she loved.

To her surprise, the girls did not seem to mind. They drew their chairs closer to the old man, plied him with questions, called for one and still another anecdote, of which he had a ready store, laughed with him, dropped their sewing to listen as he talked. Angela Seers, she noticed, seemed more interested than the rest. Even when Grandpa contradicted her flatly in the aged tone of authority, she seemed not to mind, though Priscilla leaned forward, anxiously eager to heal any breach that might occur.

Priscilla glanced about. She wondered if Angela had noticed

that awful spot in the rug, the mended curtains, the faded wallpaper. But Angela's eyes were fastened directly upon Grandpa's face while she listened intently to him.

The afternoon passed, and Priscilla disappeared kitchenward, to return presently and invite the girls to the dining-room. All rose but Grandpa, who remained seated. Angela returned to him.

"Aren't you coming?" she asked. The old man shook his head.

"I guess you've had enough of an old man for today," he answered.

"Nonsense!" Angela turned to Cynthia Rowe. "Play something, Cynthia, and we'll all march out. And Grandpa and I will lead."

Cynthia struck the opening chords of a march, and Angela slipped her arm into Grandpa's and led the way to the dining-room. The old man grinned and chuckled, expostulating all the way, and yet with no wish to turn back. His eyes twinkled. His flush deepened. Once in the dining-room, he did the honors well. He found a place for Angela on the window seat and served her as gallantly as though he too were eighteen instead of eighty. He was having a wonderful time. Once when Priscilla passed, he caught her dress eagerly.

"I wasn't comin' out, Prissy," he said apologetically, "but Angie here, she wouldn't hear to my stayin' back."

"Of course I wouldn't," returned Angela. "I wouldn't have come without you."

Soothed and pleased, Grandpa again felt that he could enjoy the company, and he made the most of the privilege.

The girls had nearly all gone. Only a few loitered in the rooms upstairs to finish bits of conversation started earlier in the afternoon. Priscilla stood in the lower hall waiting. She was keenly aware, now that the sun was low and its glow did not light up the rooms with its kindly rays, that their shabbiness was more evident than ever. Most of all, she felt that the keen eyes of Angela Seers, who was just then coming downstairs, would detect their shabbiness more plainly.

She was feeling tired; it was the reaction from her many emotions. In the living-room the fire burned low, and Grandpa had moved over to one of the sagging chairs with its comfortable hollows. Voices from above drifted to her ears. Angela paused on the landing and called down to her.

"Don't move, Priscilla. I want you right there just as you are. You too, Grandpa," as the old man started to turn in his chair. "It's like some beautiful picture, and I want to feast my eyes. You don't appreciate, I'm sure, Priscilla, what a beautiful home you have. It has so much atmosphere, so much of the true home spirit. And Grandpa," she said, smiling at the old man, "Grandpa has a large part in it. I've always wanted a little house like this with a grandfather in it. You just don't know how rich you are." She stepped down from the landing and stood at Priscilla's side. "I'm planning to have you both come to lunch some day next week. My aunt will love to hear Grandpa tell about the old town."

The last guests had gone. Priscilla turned from the door to the living-room. It had the usual upset air following an afternoon of company. Grandpa watched her for a few moments as she pushed chairs into place, straightened books and magazines on the table, and pulled down the shades.

"That Angie Seers," he said finally, when there was a lull in Priscilla's operations. "I feel right sorry for her. She hasn't what you can rightly call a home. They've a house in New York, and a country place on Long Island, and they spend their summers, what's left of 'em when they aren't travelin' in furrin parts, at their cottage at the seashore. That's the only one that sounds a little bit like a home—the cottage. An' like as not, if we come to see it, we'd think 'twas a town hall. I don't wonder she enjoyed spendin' the afternoon with us in this house, Prissy. It's about as near to bein' a home as anything I know."

Priscilla stared at her grandfather for a moment bewilderedly. She had not thought of it in that light before. Three homes, and the intervals spent in traveling about. Grandpa was right. Angela hadn't any real home, even such a shabby little home as this. She glanced about the room. The fire sent bright tongues upward, the clock ticked softly, the worn place on the rug revealed itself as a blotch of gray in the waning light. But it had been made, she knew, by the passing of many feet that entered the door of the little house from time to time and felt that they had come home.

She seated herself on the arm of her grandfather's chair.

"You're right, Grandpa," she said. "This is a shabby little house, but it's a real home."

"Course it is, Prissy," he replied, encircling her lovingly within his arm. "But just remember, too, it's the people in the house that make it a home, no matter what the shell of the house is really like. Angie, she sensed that," he said, a little wistfully. "She seemed to like to have me here."

Priscilla bent and kissed the withered cheek.

"So do I, Grandpa," she said softly. "And after all," she added, "if it hadn't been for you, the party wouldn't have been such a success. Every girl told me she had spent the pleasantest afternoon she could remember for a long while. And they meant it, I know they did. There wasn't one bit of pretense about it."

"I s'pose 'tis a shabby little house," replied Grandpa, "but I tell you, where the love an' the true home spirit are piled on thick enough, not a bit of the shabbiness shows. No, sir; not a bit of it."

Irene S. Woodcock

Irene S. Woodcock wrote for family and inspirational magazines early in the twentieth century.

THE SUPER-DUPER

Mary Kay Thompson

So little money, so many grandchildren. And she wanted to give special gifts this year. So what could she do to get through Christmas?

Three more grandchildren in high school this year. I just don't know what to do about Christmas gifts. It was easier when they were all small."

I sat talking with my friend Sarah Wescott at the Harvest Fair. "There's so little money and I hate to disappoint them, and—" I sighed—"I've made Jim a sweater almost every year since we've been married."

Sarah looked surprised. "As good a cook and seamstress as you are, whatever can be the problem?"

"I'm tired of giving the boys homemade shirts and the girls blouses. And poor Jim couldn't wear all the sweaters if we were married for another fifty years." I sat and poked at a few crumbs on the table. "I'd like to give them all something really big, I guess. Something, as Jonathan says, 'super-duper.' "

"Well, Rachel," Sarah laughed, "knowing you, you'll think of something." She stood up and took the cups.

I wandered over to Grannie Johnson's table in the church hall, always so cleaned and scrubbed with the whitewashed walls and the blue-and-white checkered gingham curtains that we'd all helped sew. I stopped at the small window and reached up and fingered the soft cloth. These curtains were ten years old now, almost time for a change. *These were made the year Betsy was born,* I thought, and I remembered I had made a sunsuit and a bonnet for her out of the scraps.

Grannie Johnson called to me, "Rachel, whatever are you doing standing there, smiling to beat all?"

"Oh, Grannie, I guess I'm just remembering when these were made and what I'd done with the scraps." I smiled at her and started helping her load up the few things that hadn't sold. "I made a sunsuit and bonnet for Betsy, Bill's youngest, out of some of the curtain scraps."

Grannie thought for a minute. "It was the winter Rev. Ridgefield got called to the new church and we spent a lot of evenings making a memory quilt for him and Mrs. Ridgefield to take with them."

"Land, yes, Grannie, I had forgotten. You still have the best memory in the parish."

We started to pick up the patchwork pot holders and pack the few that remained. Grannie reached for a Dresden one, all made in different lovely scraps of blue. "See this one, this is a scrap from John's shirt, and this is from Deborah's first long dress, and this," she said, pointing, "is from Jennie's Easter Bunny costume in the class play. It's a nice way to use all the scraps I save from the things I make during the year for the great-grandchildren."

"What a nice idea. The potholders are like a scrapbook full of memories," I said, and then excused myself.

Sarah and I folded the last of the craft tables and checked the stoves, and then I headed home.

I couldn't wait to get in the house. I had an idea for a special gift for each member of the family, but before I let myself get too excited, I had to check the sewing corner and the storage closet.

"Home, Jim," I called to let him know it was me.

"You're early. Like a cup of tea? How was the supper?"

"No tea, thanks. But the supper was fine." Jim smiled and wandered back into the living room to watch TV.

I turned out the kitchen lights before I stopped by Jim's chair and kissed him goodnight. At his raised eyebrows, I said, "I've got something I want to do in my sewing nook. And I've got a busy day tomorrow."

I went upstairs to my sewing corner and started opening boxes I pulled from the storage bin, especially those marked "trims and scraps for doll clothes." Smiling when I saw how many I had, I went off to bed.

As soon as Jim left the next morning and I had done the chores, I called the catalog store and ordered the few things I needed for my Christmas presents. *There's plenty,* I thought, *and I have just about enough time to finish them.*

Later Jim teased me about the amount of time I was spending upstairs. "Rachel, I haven't seen you in such a flurry of sewing since Becky's wedding dress and trousseau. Whatever are you working on?"

"It's a secret and a surprise. If I tell you, the kids will wheedle it out of you." I laughed and waved my ruler at him. "You stay out of my sewing corner and I'll stay out of your workshop."

"That's a deal! And you've got to promise not to use any of my screwdrivers to mix paint with." He ducked as I threatened him with my ruler. The screwdriver-as-a-paint-stirrer incident had happened the first year we were married, and he'd never let me forget it.

Christmas Eve came, and everything was finished! I wrapped them in white tissue and put brightly colored ribbons and bits of trim on them. Two by two, I carried them down to the big tree in the parlor. There was one for everybody—fifteen fat, plump, cushiony boxes.

Jim had carved each of the family a songbird, perched them on beautifully polished bases of apple wood, and put them by the plates on the table. Mine was a tiny bluebird.

"The bluebird is the nicest of all," he told me. "It means happiness and that's you." Jim twinkled. "That's *us.*"

After Christmas Eve supper, we all gathered around the tree drinking tea and eating slices of fruitcake. Jim called out the names on the boxes, beginning with the youngest, and soon the parlor was a mass of ribbons and tissue and talking. One by one, the memory quilts were unwrapped, and the family was laughing and sharing.

"Hey, my baseball uniform!"

"My first long dress! My wedding dress; oh, Mom!"

"My blouse. Grannie, my graduation dress! Oh, I'd forgotten this!"

And from Jonathan, "Wow, a memory quilt. Super-duper, Gram!"

But best of all was the acknowledgment from Jim as he reached for my hand. Jim's quilt had a square for each of the years we were married, and on the first one I had embroidered a bride with a stove, a groom with a toolbox, and in the corner, a small paint-stained screwdriver. Each square had a memory of a special time we had shared together.

Jim squeezed my hand and swallowed. "I thought you'd made me at least six sweaters, in that box. But, Rachel," Jim swallowed again, "Jonathan is right! It's . . . it's a super-duper gift!"

Mary Kay Thompson

Mary Kay Thompson wrote for family magazines during the second half of the twentieth century.

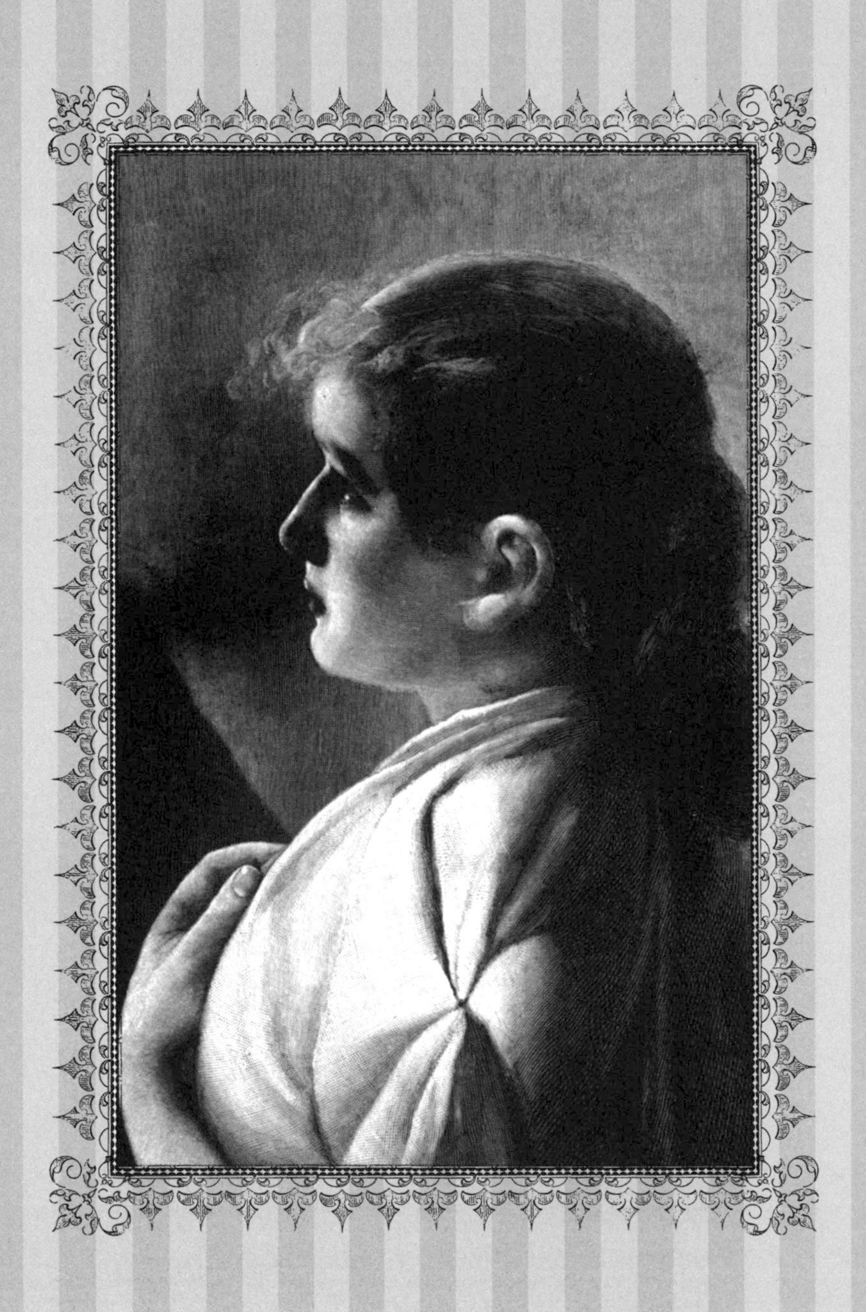

THIS WAS MY SON

Avis Dungan

This is a grandparent story like none I have ever read before. The setting: a small American town during World War II. The protagonists: a woman who thought she had already experienced all the pain life could bring her, and a much younger woman, a city girl, who had just come into town.

Then there they were: two identical telegrams.

Kate Bryant slid her chair back from the breakfast table and got up with an effort. Since the telegram had come four days ago, every move had cost effort. By willing and thinking hard she had managed to get down some coffee and a slice of toast. Now she must will and think again in order to put on her wraps.

Biggsie had them ready, her homely old face broken with compassion.

"You mustn't spoil me, Biggsie," Kate said gratefully, and felt her throat grow tighter. The words were an old family joke. Long ago Stephen had uttered them gravely when the new maid had proffered a service he felt beneath his three-year-old dignity.

Kate swayed dizzily in her pain. Everything stabbed her with remembrance these days. Even the name "Biggsie" reminded her: "Mother, do you think she'd mind it? 'Mrs. Biggerton' is sort of long when you want *in.*"

"After a while it won't hurt so bad."

"I don't know, Biggsie. Do you remember once you told me—it was the time he had pneumonia and I was so tired and afraid—that when a woman brings a child into the world she writes a blank check on her life and can't know when nor for how much it will be filled in? I'm finding that the toughest payment of all is knowing there are no more."

"It's the God's truth, dearie, but you're a strong, brave woman and you can pay it better than most."

"I'm a very weak sister this morning," Kate said dully.

On the doorstep the sharp December wind stung against her face. She decided against driving. The effort would be too great. There was no hurry. The paper would come out whether she appeared at the office or not. "It may not be the best county seat paper in the state," she had once boasted, "but it has the most dependable staff."

Nothing really needed her any more, she thought, breasting the wind and indifferent to it.

Even with the ravages of the last week upon her, Kate Bryant was a good-looking woman. She had contrived to make the gray threads standing out unabashed against the sleek black of her hair give her a touch of downright distinction. Her shoulders were square and her head sat on them straight and high. In all her life she had never carried a pound of surplus flesh or calculated a calorie. When women envied her for it, she laughed. "I've never been still long enough for a pound to take roost."

It was perfectly true. When young Jim Bryant had died in the great flu epidemic, he had left her only a baby boy and a debt-bogged country weekly. She had just turned twenty-three then and had never held a job in her life.

In the first years she had known what it was to stand off creditors who swore they would have their money on the spot and to pry subscriptions out of farmers who swore they had no money. She had taken her turn, in those days, at every job in the little plant. Once when the linotype operator went on a three-day binge, she had even struggled all night over his machine and emerged at dawn with her paper set.

She had carried her share of the community's burden, too. Carrying it was a necessity in her business, but she would have done it anyway, for, as she often said, she wanted Stephen to grow up in a good town. Somewhat to the scandal of other women she had made herself a place in the Chamber of Commerce. She had been on the school board and had her finger in all the better political pies of the region. By the grim process of letting her knees knock until they stopped of their own accord, she had learned to speak in public. For years now it had been almost a part of the week's routine to shoot her car out along fifty or a hundred miles of pavement and make a speech in some town or consolidated schoolhouse.

Through it all she had found time for Stephen—to spin tops and fly kites with him when he was a little boy, to hike and skate with him later, to take carloads of his high school gang to out-of-town football games and stuff them with hot dogs afterward, to cultivate some comprehension of swing, and to run down for weekends with him when he was in the state university.

As she moved down the familiar flat streets and around the familiar corners, everything hurt her.

A group of schoolboys stared solemnly at her, and one or two of the most mannerly touched their caps. A week ago, she knew, they would merely have tossed off a "Hi-ya, Mrs. Bryant." Two weeks ago one of them might have sung out, "Say, Mrs. Bryant, where's Steve's outfit now? . . . Pearl Harbor? Hot diggety!"

At the filling station, Bill Horton rose from the tire he was testing. He wiped off his hand and extended it awkwardly. "I just want you to know, Mrs. Bryant, that we all feel for you. Steve was the swellest fella I ever knew. All the things they said about him at the memorial service yesterday were true. Betty and I were talking last night that we never knew him to do anything that wasn't on the level and out in the open."

Kate squeezed his grimy young hand and thanked him dumbly. For four days now these tributes had been coming in. The note with the Governor's roses had said, "In memory of one of the cleanest-cut young Americans it has been my privilege to meet." But every time one of them came it melted her down completely. Some day, perhaps, she would be able to thank people properly for their kindness.

She walked on, thinking dully.

A pretty girl in sweater and slacks looked down from the porch she was sweeping and smiled. There was a time, Kate knew, when Becky Rivers would have given her eyeteeth for Stephen, and not only Becky. Half the girls in town had pitted their wits and their wiles against him. *He had been a match for them, though,* Kate thought with a touch of the old, amused pride. *He had liked them and beaued them around but kept them on a strictly light emotional diet.* Having braced herself to deal with adolescent agony, Kate had been delighted, and proud, at its non-appearance. "It only goes to show," she had told herself, "what happens when you give a youngster your time and understanding."

Walking along slowly, she thought of all the old mother-of-a-son anxieties, now so far away and pointless. The one time when she had thought she detected a serious note in him was about the dancer he had met the first time he spent his day off from camp in New York. And that was only for one letter. In her reply she had reminded him humorously that when a country boy turns Stage-door Johnny, he'd better watch his step. He had not referred to the girl again. So it was nothing, after all.

Occasionally during the last years, when so much was being written about the danger of mothers and sons being too close, she had been vaguely uneasy. Now she was glad. In death he had returned to her, as he used to return when he wore knickers, whole, with no links dragging from his small excursions away from her.

She reached the plant at last.

"You shouldn't have tried to come down so soon, Mrs. Bryant," protested Harriet, the office girl of all work.

"I had to start sometime, and, smart as you all are, there must be a few things which nobody else but me can do."

"Oh, there are, a hundred or two of them, only I've put most of them in the cooler, where they'll keep."

Kate heard her dimly. She was looking at the live young face in the silver frame on her desk. The picture was new, made on his last weekend in New York. "To Mom with all my love," he had printed across the uniformed shoulder.

Presently she sat down at her desk and began to finger listlessly through the four-day accumulation on it. Bills. Receipts. A lot of hand-addressed envelopes—they would contain more of the tributes which smote her with such pride and pain. She laid them aside until she should feel more equal to them.

She stared helplessly at the litter. It looked mountain-huge and there was no will in her to attack it. After a while she called in Harriet. "You said you had put most of them in the cooler. What wouldn't go in?"

"Well, they want to know if you'll go on with your chairmanship of the Red Cross. The organization has to be got together for the big new drive for funds. And there's that meeting about the school lunch program that was scheduled for Monday. You were to speak, you know, and it seems nobody else has the facts and figures in hand."

Kate shivered. These were decisions which had to be made, for if she slipped out of harness someone would have to be found to take her place. "I don't know, Harriet, I'll think about it till afternoon. I feel so slack."

❧

At midmorning Harriet came in looking troubled. "There's a girl out here who says she has to see you. She won't tell me what she wants."

"Who is she?"

"Nobody I ever saw before. She's very pretty and she sounds eastern. She says her name is Thelma Green and she *has* to see you."

"Let her come in."

Even when she was in the room, Kate felt no warning rise within her. She scarcely felt even the ordinary excitement of a human being confronted with another human being completely foreign to her experience. At another time her newswoman's eye would have taken in at a glance the piquantly irregular features, the round throat, and the smooth muscled legs. She would have noted the warm, creamy skin and the lustrous brown eyes framed by a shining gold bob. She would have appraised the groomed eyebrows and odd shade of lipstick. She would have seen that the fur jacket and matching toque were not expensive and the pumps not new. Today she saw only enough to make her think indifferently, *We don't grow them like that around here.*

She seated the girl and waited for her to speak.

"I am Thelma Green, Mrs. Bryant." The young body sat tensely erect and the eyes bored straight into Kate's.

"I'm sorry, but I can't place you. Are you the daughter of someone I have known?"

"Maybe, then, you know me as Lona Lanier?"

Puzzling vaguely over the unfamiliar accent and speech rhythm, Kate started to say no again. Then she remembered. Her numbed senses stirred sharply, and something deep and primitive within her went on the defensive. *This can't be. It only happens in novels,* she thought desperately.

Her first reaction was to spar for time. "Lona Lanier," she said slowly. "I don't believe—"

But the girl harried her out quickly: "Oh, surely he wrote you about me. He told me he did."

"Let me think. Are you by any chance the dancer he mentioned once?"

The girl winced, but she said quietly, "Whenever he could be in New York he came to see me at the little café where I dance."

"My son liked you very much," Kate said slowly, thinking of Stephen's words—the words she had read so many times in the effort to feel out what lay behind them: "She makes me think of you, Mom, though of course she looks nothing like you. She's a spunky kid, who knows where she wants to go and won't ask anybody for a lift."

"He loved me, Mrs. Bryant." The accent fell calmly on the second word.

Kate was now fully in possession of herself. What was the game of this girl? The affair couldn't have meant anything or Stephen would have continued to write about it. He had always talked easily and voluminously about his girls.

"You know what has happened?" she asked.

"Yes, I know. That's why I came. It seemed to me I had to see the place he lived in, and you. I had so little of him." The words came evenly, as if they had been rehearsed. The brown eyes were dry and deep.

A wave of anger shook Kate. *The nerve of her, pushing in at such a time.*

"I don't quite understand, Miss Lanier. Stephen mentioned you in only one letter. Naturally, I had not supposed—"

"Young men don't always tell their mothers everything."

"But Stephen and I were unusually close."

"He told me so. Once he said he couldn't stand it if you and I didn't like each other. Another time he said that we had such awful hurdles between us that he didn't want us to start with any prejudices got from something he might say."

"Hurdles?"

"I think he meant the difference between our ages, and our belonging to different parts of the country, and you being his mother and I his—"

"His?"

"The girl he was going to marry." The words came out with a catch of defiance.

Kate's world trembled. If someone had told her that he had spent half his training period in the guardhouse she would not have been more startled or disbelieving. Stephen wouldn't have talked marriage without being in love, and he wouldn't have been shaken by the experience of love without confiding in her. He couldn't have. It wasn't in character. Bill Horton's remark came back to fortify her: *We never knew him to do anything that wasn't on the level and out in the open.*

"But why would he not tell me if things had gone so far between you?" *Keep your hackles down. She can't be telling the truth.*

"I wouldn't know that. After all, we weren't together much, and when we were, there were so many things to talk about. But you don't have to take my word for the engagement. I had official notice, and you know I wouldn't have got it if he had not entered my name on his record so that I would get it." She snapped open her purse and drew out a telegram.

Kate stared at it. It was like her own in every respect except for the word "fiancée." *Oh, Stephen, Stephen, why did you not tell me?*

⁂

She felt herself slipping back into the blurred slackness of the last days and fought at it frantically. Summoning up all her power to think, she saw the situation clearly. Stephen, in his youth and inexperience, had been taken in by a girl whose profession was attraction. And now she was here looking over his town and his mother appraisingly.

At the thought, Kate turned swiftly down another painful trail. With a small-town woman's intimate feeling for the backdrop against which all of her personal dramas must be played, she faced the town. If this girl chose to tell her story to anyone in it, the luster of Stephen's memory would be diminished. The story would float endlessly over shop counters and across dining tables. The very people who had praised him most extravagantly would puzzle most keenly over his uncharacteristic secretiveness. She couldn't bear to think of them speculating about Stephen.

Now completely on the defensive, Kate took her decision, loathing it with all her forthright soul. The girl had to be sealed off from contact with the town during the time she was in it, and there was only one way to do it.

Kate leaned forward and picked up one of the slim hands. "My dear," she said, "can you forgive me for the way I have been acting? I am not myself yet. If Stephen loved you, so will I."

The brown eyes gazed at her searchingly, but the tautness about them relaxed hardly at all. "It's all right, Mrs. Bryant. It must have been a shock, my coming here this way."

She's still trying to figure me out, thought Kate desperately. Aloud she said, "You will be my guest, of course, while you are here. I know you want to see Stephen's home and the things he did and had as he was growing up." *Biggsie is loyal and tight-mouthed. She can be trusted.*

For the first time the throaty young voice broke slightly: "He was right. You are wonderful."

Just then Kate heard Harriet close the door of the outer office and knew that she was going to the bank. Now was the time to get the girl out without being obliged to introduce her.

"You must be tired from your trip, and I'm not much good here today. Suppose we go out to the house now, Lona—or shall I call you Thelma?"

"He liked 'Thelma.' Once he said it made me his home-town girl."

"Then it's 'Thelma' for me, too." *We're both saying the right things. It's a duel. But I'm the one whom every scratch hurts.*

She chose a roundabout way home, ostensibly to point out the building where Stephen had gone to grade school and the pool where he had learned to swim. The girl looked at them without comment. But when they came to the house with gleaming white paint, wide porch, and clipped evergreens, she said slowly, "I thought it would be like this, fresh and plenty of room around it. I grew up in a third-floor walk-up in Brooklyn close to the el."

Lunch was difficult. Neither could eat much. Their talk was constantly of Stephen. But it was only a dialogue, or rather only two monologues fronting each other across a wide gulf. Each spoke, paused for the other to speak, replied in the proper syllables. There was no fusion, either in words or spirit.

After lunch Kate took her up to Stephen's room. It was a big, comfortable place where furniture-battering boys from the whole neighborhood had once made headquarters. His graduation present had been a new suite of limed oak. But he had insisted on keeping the old wing chair in which they had sat together with a picture book across their knees. Kate pointed it out dutifully. She opened the closet door and showed his clothes still hanging where he had left them when he went into uniform. She lifted his scrapbooks out of the bureau drawer, feeling as if she were defiling them. Through it all the girl was composed and almost silent.

They spent a long time in the room. Through her pain Kate felt a mounting uncertainty. One instant she would bitterly resent the girl's composure for the advantage it gave her. The next she would think exultantly that it proved indifference: *Girls don't act this way when they lose their lovers. He was nothing to her, after all.* But the next instant she would be uncertain and confused again. There was something elusive about the girl. And something waiting.

From the last drawer Kate took out some of his college things, his last yearbook, his honor key, a picture of his fraternity house.

The girl looked at it all carefully, and gave it back without a word.

Then she asked, slowly, as if she found it hard to say, "Do you have some pictures of him when he was a baby?"

Kate felt tormented. This was one set of mementos she had resolved not to share. Surely she had a right to that much of him by herself. But, having gone so far, there seemed no way to retreat without arousing the girl's antagonism. After all, every woman lays away baby pictures.

"They're in my desk in the living-room. We'll go down, if you're ready."

She had not dared get out this bundle of photographs during

the past four days. Times without number she had thought of them and longed to look at them, but somehow she had not had the strength. She wished now that she had done it, so that she would not have had to share the moment.

Downstairs again, she drew out a big pile of photographs and began to arrange them in order on the top of the desk. Three months, six months, one year, eighteen months, and after that one for each Christmas, down to his high-school graduation picture.

Thelma stood looking silently down at them. Presently she picked up the six-months picture and held it with an odd cuddling movement. It was a usual enough picture of a chubby baby with a curl and one hand lifted to slap a ball gripped between both feet. But the girl looked at it as if she had never seen such a picture.

At last she laid it down and lifted her face. Kate was shocked to see that her lips were quivering and her eyes burning with petition.

"I've been trying to think how to tell you all day, but there just isn't any good approach to it. I'm in trouble, Mrs. Bryant."

"In trouble?" Kate asked blankly. Somehow the homely idiom did not get to her.

"Yes. That last time he was in New York—we were trying to be so sensible and wait to get married until he would be home with a job. I wanted a wedding and he wanted us to come out and see you, so we decided to wait. And then the night before he left—"

All the animosity which she had been keeping on leash and decking in politeness flamed up in Kate. "Frankly, I don't believe it."

"But it's true."

"Stephen was too decent to let a girl he loved take a risk like that. He was fine and straight in his dealings with people. Only this morning a friend of his said he never knew him to do anything that wasn't on the level."

"I know. That's why I loved him."

After the stilted silence of the day the words tumbled out wildly: "Oh, I'm sorry to do this to you at this time, but he was your son and I thought you'd want to—"

"But how can I know it is Stephen's child? With a girl like you—" She drove into the phrase all the indignant scorn she had been feeling all day.

The brown eyes blazed. "Don't you talk to me like that. If you hadn't kept him tied to you so that he couldn't marry until you could pass judgment on me, we'd have been married. I didn't care so much about a wedding that I wouldn't have been willing to give it up."

"After all, he was pretty young and inexperienced in the situation."

"You think he was still a child. He was twenty-three years old. I'm two years younger and I've been on my own for four years."

"It seems to me that perhaps you are showing up what you really are—a girl who was on the make and got caught." Kate's voice was icy. She hated this girl. As she had never hated another human being.

"All right, if that's how you feel about it. I took a chance on coming out here, thinking you might like to know you're going to have a grandchild. All the way out I kept praying you might be one of the big-natured, motherly women one reads about, who can be kind. But all day I've known it was no good. You've loved Stephen and nothing else—and so his death is going to smash you. I'm going now." She paused slightly, then flung out, "You may keep your nice boy, Mrs. Bryant. But I had the man, and now I've got all that's alive of him on this earth."

For the first time in her life Kate Bryant fainted. She had no warning. The gray looseness of the past days simply deepened and sucked her down.

She came back up slowly. The first weary lifting of her eyelids showed that she was on the divan. She rested a moment, assembling herself. Presently she was aware of a sound. She exerted herself to listen and then to open her eyes again. The girl had her back toward her. She was sitting before the desk, sobbing.

Kate rested again. Out of the far past, words returned: "You kept him tied to you." She turned them over gently, like beads slipping on a thread. Had she? She hadn't meant to. Or had she? No matter now. Anyway, the tie had been strong. So strong that Stephen had had to sever it in silence and stealth. How he must have suffered!

The soft rhythm by the desk continued. Kate let her thoughts waver on. *Poor child, so young. Like herself, so long ago, young and a baby to fend for. It would be worse for this girl with no wedding ring and no small, friendly town at her back. Much worse.*

She took another languid look, and her eyes fell on the girl's shoes. Practically worn out. Probably not ten dollars in her purse. And she'd not be able to dance much longer.

More words floated back: "You loved only Stephen, so now his death is going to smash you." She was already smashed.

"Grandchild . . . all that is alive of him." Something of him still loved and needed her!

Her eyelids sprang wide open and she lifted her head with a sudden rush of strength.

At the sound the girl dabbed at her eyes and came over beside her. "Feeling better?"

"Much better. I'm glad you're still here."

"I thought probably you wouldn't want anybody to know what a turn I had given you, and I couldn't go off and leave you alone."

"I'm sorry I went out on you like that."

"I was pretty nasty."

Kate pulled herself up to a sitting position. "Listen to me, Thelma—don't you dare lift anyone to a divan while you're carrying my grandchild. If someone faints, let her lie."

The girl smiled moistly.

"As for your being nasty, I deserved it. In fact, it's a mercy you were. Otherwise I might never have understood how stupid I've been.

"And now, about this problem of yours," she went on. "Did you have anything in mind that I could do?"

"I'm afraid not. But Stephen was always so sure you could manage anything that I had to try you."

"There are plenty of things I can't manage, one being myself, but this happens to be a situation right down my alley. I have this house and no one to share it with. I run a newspaper where there are always jobs to be done. And I know everyone in this town. You can live here with me, and I'll introduce you to everyone and make sure they know it's my grandchild you're carrying."

"But will people accept me?"

"No doubt a few mean souls will gossip, but I'll back you up. After a while the talk will die down and they'll learn to love you the way they loved Stephen."

Thelma began to cry again, this time in the full, luxurious sobs of a woman who is safe at home and can at long last let go.

When Kate perceived that it was going to be a long session, she picked up the telephone from the table beside her.

"Harriet," she said, still a little weak and breathless, "will you notify the Red Cross people that I'm not resigning and the superintendent that I'll be on hand Monday?"

Avis Dungan

Avis Dungan wrote for popular magazines early and mid-twentieth century.

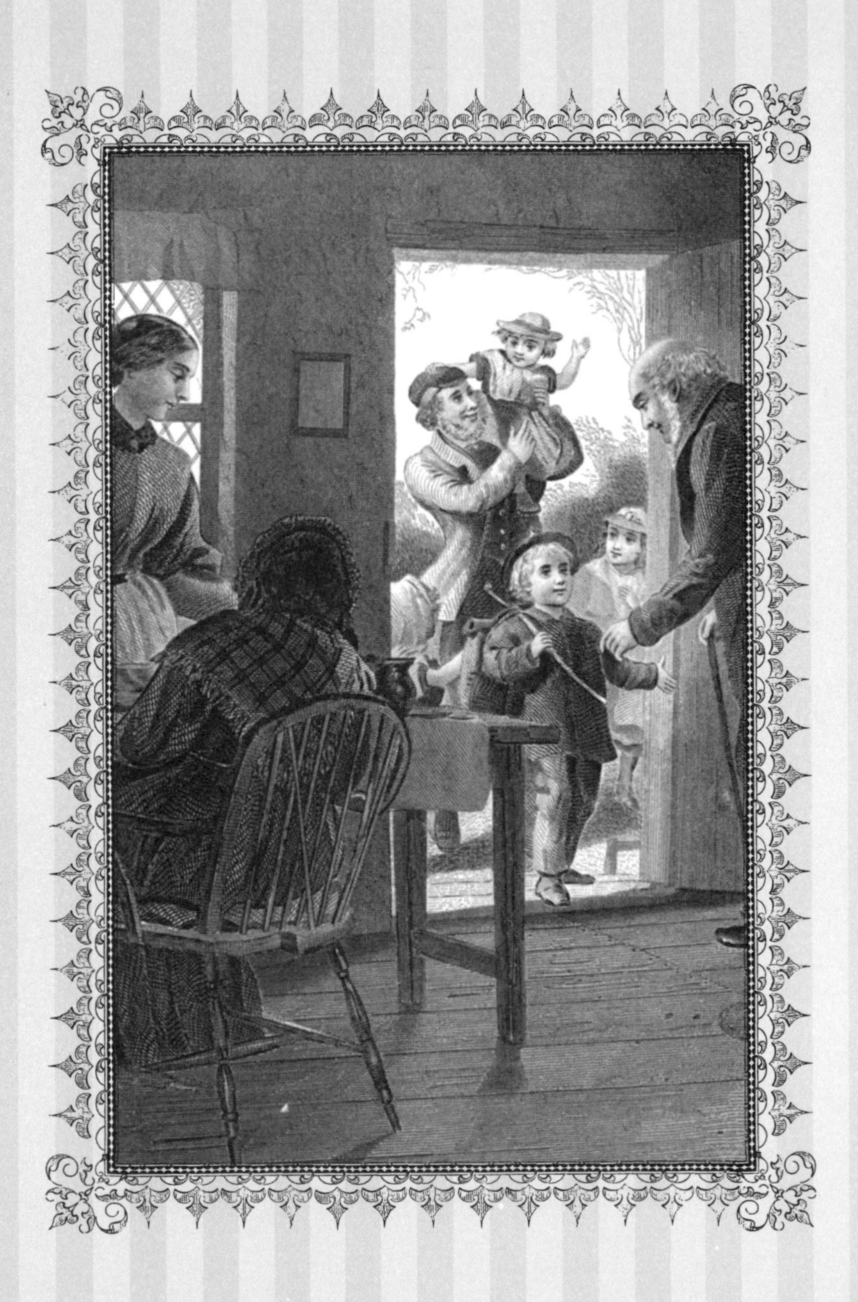

LEGACY

Joseph Leininger Wheeler

Just what is a legacy? Is it a masterpiece created by a great painter or sculptor? Is it a villa by the sea? Is it a treasure chest of rare gems? Is it stocks and bonds worth millions?

Or could it be something entirely different?

It was cold and foggy that bleak December day on the Oregon coast. But inside my aunt's farmhouse living room it was cheery, and a hot fire crackled in the big black iron stove. On the mantel was a stack of Christmas cards and letters, and in a corner stood a small Christmas tree.

Suddenly, around the corner stalked Mr. Tibbs, a proud old tomcat of venerable years and uncertain ancestry. But lack of pedigree had never bothered Mr. Tibbs; in fact, he reveled in his mongrel polyglot Americanism. *He* would establish the dynasty.

Called upon by my aunt to perform for me, Mr. Tibbs leisurely responded in his own good time, letting me know he condescended to do so not because I was in any respect worthy of it, but because he owed my aunt one of his royal favors. Old as he was, he hesitated before he wheezed his way to the stool-top, licked his chops at the cheese my aunt held high above him, and then stood up tall on his back legs to claim the prize, never for a moment losing his dignity.

After Mr. Tibbs had paid his dues, he descended from the stool and swaggered out.

In the quiet moments that followed, I wondered, *Do I dare bring it up . . . again? Surely if she had been receptive to my plea, she would have responded long ere this. And, for good measure, my uncle hadn't responded either—and now he lies in his grave up on that misty green hill overlooking the valley. Perhaps . . . I'd just better forget it for now.* So I said nothing, and only leaned back into the softness of the couch, dozy because of the alder wood fire.

I was a boy again . . . and my heart was leaping within me because I knew we were nearing the ranch. The first gate loomed ahead, and Dad's Ford slowed and stopped so I could get out. This had always been *my* job! The long wooden bar slid back, and the heavy gate lifted and opened at last; then I stood there holding it while the Ford chugged past me and stopped.

Ever so slowly, for I was ever so small, I struggled across the road, that balky gate fighting me all the way. After reinserting the bar, I ran up to the car for the best part of all: riding on the running board to the other side of Frazzi's vineyard. Some days we'd drive up to the Frazzi house and Mrs. Frazzi, large of girth, dark of complexion, poor with her English, and robust with her belly laugh, would throw her plump arms around me, brag about how I had grown, and tow me over to the always overflowing cookie jar.

But not today. . . . Down I leaped for the second gate, also of heavy wood. It too was a struggle and resisted every inch, squawking all the way. Once again the Ford rolled past and stopped. Once again I got on the running board.

The next gate, of metal pipe and wire mesh, was easier. Overhead I could hear the wind in the pines; occasionally, we'd see a deer bounding through the manzanita, madrone, and buckbrush bushes. Today the road was dusty, but sometimes there would be snow on it instead.

On the running board again, and jolting our way ever higher up the mountain, my heart was beating so turbulently it threatened to leap out of me. At last, the big maple tree and the clearing. Thousands of apple trees to our left, and just ahead, at the top of the crest, was the walled home of the self-anointed "Old Man of the Mountain"—Grandpa Rollo, and his jolly wife, Grandma Ruby, who was deaf.

All the way up that last hill, Dad laid on the horn; as he swerved around to the house, there they were waving, Grandma saying over and over to Grandpa, "Wh-y-y-y, Papa!" and to each of us in turn, "You d-e-e-a-a-r soul!" Barking dogs provided the background sound.

Up there on top of the mountain, the seven-hundred-acre ranch stretched away—to my childish eyes, to forever. I would explore it later. First of all, though, we'd go through the gate, through the evergreen-tree windbreak behind the circular rock wall, to the little rock house in the middle. The door *always* squeaked. Inside it was rather dark, but there on the lip of the rock fireplace were the purring cats. As often as not, one of them would be leaning against the great wicker basket of blocks.

The wind would howl and the rain would pelt, but inside that snug little cabin of a house, with so much love and laughter; with the fire in the fireplace; with the kerosene lamp's soft glow; with the fragrance of homemade bread, fresh applesauce, and cold milk just feet away; with one of the cats or kittens purring on my lap; and with the blocks already stacked into dream buildings—well, it was home: it was Shangri-la.

Then we'd hear other horns, other slammed car doors, each punctuated by "Why Papa!" and "You dear souls!" Then more laughter as uncles and aunts and cousins poured into the walled enclosure.

Swirling mists blotted out the little cabin and the side house where we children stayed when we got older, with its swinging, banging doors and semiclear plastic windows instead of glass ones. Not far beyond was the outhouse, with its abridged Sears catalogue and pesky wasps.

Years passed, and we flew in silver DC3s to places thousands of miles away. Places where there were bougainvillea in the patios, royal palms bowing in rainy-season winds, freshly cut stalks of bananas on our back porch, and exhausting heat.

But every once in a blessed while, the silver birds would bring us back home, home to the three gates, the "Why, Papas", the "You dear souls," the cats on the hearth, and the blocks.

Once a new word entered my childish vocabulary. My grandfather was hauled into court by a neighboring rancher over water rights. The opposing attorney, attempting to diminish the value of Grandpa's ranch, asked the loaded question, "How much is your ranch worth?"

Grandpa's attorney, never missing a beat, stepped in and shot a question back: "Do you mean the value if it came on the real estate market? Or do you mean its *esoteric* value?" *Esoteric* was a big word for me, but after I looked it up in the dictionary and had Mom explain it, I thoroughly understood. The esoteric value was the greatest view in all the Napa Valley region, the multihued sunsets, the fog banks rolling in from the Pacific, the snow flocking the evergreens and apple trees, the little walled house on the mountaintop, the thoughts, the dreams. . . . Oh, how—how could one possibly put a value on all that? Ah yes, it was easy for me to grasp the attorney's question, for children value esoterically to begin with.

A door slammed, and I was jerked out of the past and propelled into the present. I heard voices: my aunt was needed down at the barn. . . . Then there was silence again, and once again I slipped backwards into time.

A number of years had passed and Grandpa and Grandma were growing old. The winters at the top of the mountain were hard and cold. The apple business was exhausting. Then came the news: the big ranch was sold, and they were moving down the mountain to a smaller (eighty-acre) place.

The next time we went to see them, we came to their one gate only a short distance off the paved road. There was a larger compound now, surrounded by a long mesh fence to keep the deer out. Initially there was only a tiny cabin there, but over time Grandpa built a big, beautiful brick home—a veritable palace compared to the older one! Out the broad picture windows, one could look across the valley to a small lake. There were rocks and boulders everywhere, but Grandma Ruby determined (now that the children were grown and gone, now that the apple ranch had been sold) to transform her little piece of earth into a flowering paradise.

It would prove a never-ending task, and Grandma would have to wrestle like Jacob for every blossom, for every lacy fern, for every rosebud. Now when we honked and drove in, scattering cats and kittens in our wake, chances were we'd have to get out of the car, search out the business end of the hose, and tap her on the shoulder before we'd hear "Why, you dear soul!"—and, looking over our shoulders, "Why, Papa!"

Then we'd haul our suitcases into the big new house. Inside, it was spotlessly clean—it was kept that way. And it was easy to do so because, to Grandma and Grandpa, the new house was too grand to live in. They compromised by installing an iron stove in the garage and moving in there. The main house was reserved for the family: all nine surviving children and their throngs of grandchildren. Grandpa now did most of the cooking (the applesauce and nut bread) in the tiny little cabin, for Grandma had traded cooking for flowers. The beautiful kitchen in the main house was generally used only when company came.

When we'd come into the big house, there in the large family room was the great fireplace, and there on the hearth would be the wicker basket of blocks. There were never any other toys, just the blocks. As a child, I never really examined them or wondered how old they were—I just played with them. When my other cousins wandered in, they'd plunk themselves down on the floor and play with me.

As we got older, however, the siren call of horseshoes drew us outside to where those authority figures, the men, were challenging each other, trying to beat Grandpa. To us, a rite of passage was reached when we were deemed old enough to play. Every Thanksgiving, as the clan gathered from far and near, the clang of horseshoes could be heard all day long, except for during dinner when we all gathered around the long, groaning trestle table in the big house. Around it we saw a side of our parents we never saw anywhere else, for here they were still considered children by Grandpa and Grandma.

And how Grandpa loved to tell stories: stories like the one where my cousin Billy sidled up to Grandpa in the orchard and drawled, "G-r-a-n-d-p-a . . . , I t-h-i-n-k I s-e-e a-a-a s-n-a-k-e." And, as Grandpa would tell it, he'd always counter, "Now, Billy, don't tell lies! You *know* there's no snake around today."

There'd be silence for a while, until Billy forgot about the admonition and sidled up to Grandpa, saying: "G-r-a-n-d-p-a, I t-h-i-n-k I s-e-e a-a-a s-n-a-k-e," and again Grandpa would warn him not to tell lies, and again Billy would subside.

Then, Grandpa would grin as for the third time he'd hear, "G-r-a-n-d-p-a, I t-h-i-n-k I—I SEE A SNAKE!" And, no matter how many times we'd heard the story, we'd jump a foot off our chairs when Grandpa'd galvanize into frightened little boy action.

He told other stories, like the one about a man who used to take a shortcut home, from time to time, through a graveyard. Well, one dark and moonless night, he was walking through on the way home—and, unbeknownst to him, earlier that day a new grave had been dug for a funeral the following day. Well, here he came—*pad, pad, pad*—and suddenly there was no path, and *whumpf,* he plunged into the open grave. After he got up and gathered his wits, he realized where he was and tried to climb out, but it was too deep. So he called out for help, loud and long, but no one could hear him. Finally, exhausted, he gave up and sat down in one corner to wait for morning.

By this time in the story, tingles would be going up our spines as we waited for the next line. "Suddenly, he heard someone coming—*pad, pad, pad*—and *whumpf, another* man fell in!" Pausing to make sure he still had his audience, Grandpa then proceeded to tell us that the newcomer, as had been true of the first man, paced around and around the grave, trying to find a way out, but couldn't. In the pitch dark, the pacing man hadn't seen the other man crouched in a corner. Finally, the first man got up and approached the newcomer from behind, tapping him on the shoulder and saying in a sepulchral voice, "You can't make it, buddy." Then Grandpa's voice leaped into the long-awaited punch line:

"BUT HE DID!"

And we'd roar, thinking about that poor man fleeing from what he thought was a ghost. Even us kids, by now playing over by the fireplace with the blocks, would stop and listen. And stories and jokes would continue to be told . . . and we never tired of hearing them.

When there was a break in the action, Grandma would give us haircuts. In those early days, there was no motor attached to the clippers as is true today, but rather, each time Grandma squeezed the handles together, a sheaf of hair would fall. Those of us who were down the line a bit had to endure the heat generated by the ever hotter clippers; worse yet, Grandma would occasionally yank hair out by its roots—and we would howl or scream to no avail, because Grandma could not hear our wails—she could only read lips.

At night, after supper, everyone would gather round the piano and sing. Grandma would gravitate over to the piano, put her hand on the soundboard, and seraphically smile as she *felt* the music! Later yet, games would be brought out, and Grandpa would challenge all comers to caroms—and he'd whop most of his sons. If they didn't let us kids play games with them, we'd play with the blocks.

Eventually, to the sounds of slamming car doors, good-byes, shooing away cats, crunching gravel, and tears, the clan would drive away, one car at a time.

And so it went, season after season. Each time we came, before I opened the gate, I'd turn and gaze longingly up the hill towards the lost Shangri-la beyond the three gates. In all the years that followed, I could only bear to return once, but it was not the same: a multimillionaire from San Francisco lived there now and had built something at the top of the hill I cried to see.

Awareness came back to me gradually. The house was still silent, so my conscious mind picked up where I would rather not have. I remembered when it seemed best—because of the battering of the years—that Grandpa and Grandma should leave their Napa Valley garden spot and move north to Oregon so my only double relatives (my father's youngest brother, Warren, had married my mother's youngest sister, Jeannie) could be near enough to take care of them.

But now the rest of the family no longer came on holidays, and the Oregon coastal mist and rain kept Grandma inside a lot. I came to that house only twice, and each time I did so, it was not the same—not at all the same! My grandparents seemed a hundred years older than they had before. I did not see the blocks—I was too old to want to play with them anyhow. Gone was the vitality, what the Spanish call *chíspa,* that made being with them such an adventure. Then Grandpa just let go—and not too long afterward, Grandma, bereft of her lifeline into the speaking world, followed him.

By now I had a wife and children of my own, and I was far too busy to dwell much in the past. But there came a time, some years later, when I began to remember. When I belatedly realized that, of all the things our family had ever possessed, I longed for only one thing: *those blocks!* I wondered if they had by now been thrown away. Who, after all, in this hectic life we live, would care much about an ancient basket of battered-looking blocks?

It took years, though, years of wondering about those blocks along the long corridors of the night, before I posed a question in a letter to my aunt and uncle—a question I wasn't sure I wanted to hear the answer to. "Those old blocks we used to play with—if they still exist, what do you say to giving a few to each grandchild who used to play with them?" The question was rhetorical: I didn't really expect an answer . . . and I didn't get one.

But in recent days, weeks, and months, I had found myself more and more often carried back to that time so many years before, to that time when those blocks were the most important thing in the world to me, the most prized, the most *loved.* Funny how it takes so many years in life before you realize what you value: what, if the house caught on fire, you'd race for first.

I heard my aunt come in . . . and my heart began shuddering. *Did I really want to know?*

In the end, even if the blocks were gone forever, I just *had* to know!

So, struggling to keep my voice from shaking, I asked the fateful question:

"Aunt Jeannie, . . . you remember . . . uh . . . those . . . uh—"

"Ye—e—s?" she answered.

"Well, . . . it's about the . . . the . . . uh . . . *blocks* we used to play with, so many years ago. I was just curious. . . . What ever happened to them?"

Matter-of-factly, my aunt ended the uncertainty of the years: "The old blocks? They're fine. They're here."

"They're *here,* in *this house?"* I sputtered inanely.

"Yes. They're here."

Pausing to regain my equilibrium, I finally managed to say, "Uh . . . , do you mind if—*Can I see them?"*

"Of course. Come with me."

In her bedroom, in the back of her closet, was a strangely familiar brown wicker basket. Filled with old blocks. She picked it up and took it into the living room, then handed it to me.

I was so stupefied I could not talk. Lord Carnarvon himself, on first stepping into King Tutankhamen's tomb in Egypt's Valley of the Kings, could not have been more overcome than I—I, who had long since given up the blocks as lost forever!

I just stared at them stupidly, unable to say anything that made sense. Finally I sighed, "I'd almost kill for these."

My aunt smiled for the first time.

Time passed, and I continued to handle the blocks, unable to stop touching them. Finally, I asked her if she'd ever thought about my request years before.

Instantly she said that she had, and that the answer was no.

Then, seeing my woebegone face, a smile as big as Texas spread across her dear face.

"But *you* can have them, if you wish."

"If I *wish?*" I gasped out.

"Yes, but there are conditions."

"What?" I demanded.

"That they always stay together, that they are never divided, that they remain in the family *always* . . . and that—" and here her smile grew even broader—"only when you find someone who loves them as much as you do . . . can you let them go."

When I returned home with those precious blocks, I carried them with me into the passenger cabin, not daring to risk checking them on the plane.

A few days ago, for the first time in my life, I really analyzed the basket of blocks I had for so long taken for granted. The basket itself is most likely well over a century old. In it, there is an ivoryish shoe horn, a very old sock-darning egg, and an accumulation of sixty-two blocks, representing at least six generations:

- Twenty-two uncolored alphabet blocks (one, perhaps the oldest, has burn holes in each of four sides) dating back to the early 1800s. These are so old that the corners have been worn round by generations of children playing with them.

- One single *A* block, with color, dating to around the 1850s.
- Twelve multicolored picture blocks (forming a design on each side) dating back to the 1870s.
- Four very small blocks with raised figures dating back to around 1890.
- Twenty-two alphabet blocks with raised colored lettering, dating back to about 1910.
- One modern nondescript colored block dating back to the 1940s—how it got into the box I haven't the slightest idea.

Apparently, each family for over a century added blocks to the basket. Undoubtedly, a number have been lost during the family's many travels: from Massachusetts to New Hampshire to western New York to California (not long after the Civil War), then many moves crisscrossing California afterwards.

In the end, I concluded that I was glad I didn't really know for sure how old they were. It was enough that my only surviving great-aunt, memory razor-sharp in her mid-nineties, remembers playing with the blocks and thinking them "very old" even then. Are they perchance two hundred years old? I don't know. Were they played with by a distant cousin, Buffalo Bill Cody? I don't know. And the tree the oldest blocks came from? Was it standing during the Revolutionary War? Was it standing when the Pilgrims landed in 1620? I don't know . . . but it could have been.

In researching block history, I discovered that alphabet blocks date clear back to the 1600s. John Locke first advocated their use in his landmark educational book, *Some Thoughts Concerning Education,* published in 1693. Thereafter, alphabet blocks were known as "Locke's Blocks." They crossed the Atlantic and were played with by American children during Colonial times; by the mid 1800s thousands of middle- and upper-class American families owned such block sets as those earliest blocks in our family basket. Friedrich Froebel, one of the German founders of kindergarten education, urged the adoption of alphabet blocks in that curriculum, which really hit full stride in America late in the nineteenth century.[8]

But, more to the point, why do these simple little blocks mean so much to people like me? Perhaps the best answer is found in Dan Foley's wondrous book, *Toys Through the Ages:*[9] "[As] the magic land of childhood, which was filled with delight, vanished with the approach of adolescence, so, too, did the toys. Only a small fragment of the millions of toys made in times past, even during the last century, remain to bestir our nostalgia and to record the heritage of childhood." Foley then quotes Odell Shepard, who wrote in *The Joys of Forgetting,*[10] "Our toys were almost idols. There was a glamour upon them which we do not find in the more splendid possessions of our late years, as though a special light fell on them through some window of our hearts that is now locked up forever. . . . We loved them with a devotion such as we shall never feel again for any of the things this various world contains, be they ever so splendid or costly."

A few weeks ago, our grey house high in the Colorado Rockies was about as Christmassy as a house can get: on a ledge was

[8] *Andrew McClary,* Toys with Nine Lives: A Social History of American Toys *(North Haven, Connecticut: The Shoe String Press, 1997).*
[9] *Dan Foley,* Toys Through the Ages *(Philadelphia: Chilton Books, 1962).*
[10] *Odell Shepard,* The Joys of Forgetting *(Boston: Houghton Mifflin, 1929).*

Dickens's Christmas Village; on the mantel, twelve stockings; in a far corner, a tall evergreen, ablaze with ornaments and lights. Outside on the deck we had multicolored lights that could be seen from ten miles away. But for me, there was something that meant more than all these things together.

Yes, there was Taylor, our first grandchild; only seven months old, but intent on toppling the tree so that he could suck on each branch. Short of that, if he'd had his way, the lower three feet of tree would have been stripped bare of decorations. The only thing he showed comparable interest in were the blocks. He drooled on them, he sucked on them, and he took fiendish delight in swatting down the block towers we made for him. I can hear his joyful chortle yet! I would guess him to be one of the first children to have played with those blocks during the last third of a century. (Quite likely, our son Greg was one of the last to have played with them—during the late 1960s.)

So it was that as I watched Taylor play, I felt a soothing sense of the continuity of life, of the past joining hands with the present, of a long procession of ancestors magically shedding their wrinkles and beards, gray hair and hoop skirts, and all plopping themselves down on the floor with the blocks, as children once again.

As for Taylor, I wondered if he'd love them as much as *I* did, as *they* did. Probably not, for our generations (even I was a Depression baby) had very few things to play with, compared to the king's ransom in toys we shower upon children today. Which makes me think, *Perhaps we were lucky, for we appreciated what little we had.*

So it is that never can I look at this basket of blocks without memories flooding in upon me: memories of Taylor, myself, my son Greg, my father, my grandfather, and a host of faded tintype-photograph ancestors. Given that intergenerational bond, somehow it does not seem far-fetched at all to me to imagine Grandma's greeting her home-coming family in the New Earth by saying, "You *dear* soul!" to each of us, then turning to Grandpa with, "Why, Papa"—and Grandpa turning to me and saying, "Joe, . . . did you, uh . . . by any chance, bring the blocks?"

The Castle-Builder

A gentle boy with soft and silken locks
A dreamy boy, with brown and tender eyes,
A castle-builder, with his wooden blocks,
And towers that touch imaginary skies.

A fearless rider on his father's knee,
An eager listener unto stories told
At the Round Table of the nursery,
Of heroes and adventures manifold.

There will be other towers for thee to build;
There will be other steeds for thee to ride;
There will be other legends, and all filled
With greater marvels and more glorified.

Build on, and make thy castles high and fair,
Rising and reaching upward to the skies;
Listen to voices in the upper air,
Nor lose thy simple faith in mysteries.

Henry Wadsworth Longfellow

Joe Wheeler fan? Like curling up with a good story?
Try these other Joe Wheeler books that will give you
that "warm all over" feeling.

HEART TO HEART STORIES OF LOVE

Remember old-fashioned romance? The hauntingly beautiful, gradual unfolding of the petals of love, leading up to the ultimate full flowering of marriage and a lifetime together? From the story of the young army lieutenant returning from World War II to meet his female pen pal at Grand Central Station in the hope that their friendship will develop into romance, to the tale of a young woman who finds love in the romantic history of her grandmother, this collection satisfies the longing for stories of genuine, beautiful, lasting love.

Heart to Heart Stories of Love will warm your heart with young love, rekindled flames, and promises kept.
0-8423-1833-X

HEART TO HEART STORIES OF FRIENDSHIP

A touching collection of timeless tales that will uplift your soul. For anyone who has ever experienced or longed for the true joy of friendship, these engaging stories are sure to inspire laughter, tears, and tender remembrances. Share them with a friend or loved one.
0-8423-0586-6

HEART TO HEART STORIES FOR DADS

This collection of classic tales is sure to tug at your heart and take up permanent residence in your memories. These stories about fathers, beloved teachers, mentors, pastors, and other father figures are suitable for reading aloud to the family or for enjoying alone for a cozy evening's entertainment.
0-8423-3634-6

HEART TO HEART STORIES FOR MOMS

This heartwarming collection includes stories about the selfless love of mothers, stepmothers, surrogate mothers, and mentors. Moms in all stages of life will cherish stories that parallel their own, those demonstrating the bond between child, mother, and grandmother.
A collection to cherish for years to come.
0-8423-3603-6

HEART TO HEART STORIES FOR SISTERS

Heart to Heart Stories for Sisters is a touching collection of classic short stories that is sure to tug at the heartstrings and become a family favorite. These stories about sisters and the relationships that bind them together are perfect for reading aloud to the whole family, for giving to your own sister, or simply for enjoying alone.

CHRISTMAS IN MY HEART
Volume VIII

These stories will turn hearts to what Christmas—and life itself—is all about. Powerful and inspirational, each story is beautifully illustrated with classic engravings and woodcuts, making the collection a wonderful gift for family members and friends. Reading these stories will quickly become a part of any family's Christmas tradition.
0-8423-3645-1

CHRISTMAS IN MY HEART
Volume IX

From the tale of the orphan boy who loses a beloved puppy but finds a loving home for Christmas, to the narrative of an entire town that gives an impoverished family an unexpectedly joyful Christmas, these heartwarming stories will touch your soul with the true spirit of the season. Featured authors include O. Henry, Grace Livingston Hill, Margaret Sangster, Jr., and others.

Christmas is a time for families to take time to sit together, perhaps around a crackling blaze in the fireplace, and reminisce about Christmases of the past. Enjoy the classic stories found in this book and understand why thousands of families have made the Christmas in My Heart series part of their traditions.
0-8423-5189-2

CHRISTMAS IN MY HEART
Volume X

Christmas in My Heart, vol. 10 will bring a tear to your eye and warmth to your heart as you read the story of a lonely little girl who helps a heartbroken mother learn to love again, or the tale of a cynical old shop-keeper who discovers the true meaning of Christmas through the gift of a crippled man. Authors include Pearl S. Buck, Harry Kroll, Margaret Sangster, Jr., and others.
0-8423-5380-1